Marketing and promotion will include a national media
campaign, bookseller/librarian outreach, digital advertising,
targeted newsletters, social posts, and giveaways.

For more information, contact:
Rachel Fershleiser, Associate Publisher,
Executive Director of Marketing
rachel.fershleiser@catapult.co

Advance Praise for *Mothers*

"In this novel, the language twirls then leaves us with questions like open wounds: What are we mothers capable of doing for the love of a daughter? What helps–or hinders—access to social services and health systems for women? Who has access to justice? What are the consequences of fear for our society? How can we ever forgive? These questions all echo through our current context. With an engaging cast of characters and an astute narrator, Lozano knits together Mexico City in the 1940s and our contemporary moment with surprising power and tenderness."
—Gabriela Jauregui, author of *Controlled Decay*

"*We hear this is what happened* . . . This is the beginning of a novel that has the momentum of a police report and the power of a period piece. Class, motherhood, life in the city, and the media are just some of the pieces of this astonishing puzzle, this novel that seems to be speaking of the past but is actually telling us about the present."
—Mauro Libertella

Praise for *Witches*

"The biggest success of *Witches* is the way [Lozano] weaves together two distinct voices—one Spanish-speaking, from the capital, righteously angry about gender violence, and the other leaving aside the 'government's tongue' in favor of her own, matter-of-factly explaining life in rural Mexico . . . Beautifully translated."
—Rachel Nolan, *The New York Times Book Review*

"Set in Mexico, this is a layered, kaleidoscopic and powerful story exploring relationships, fluidity, pain, healing, power and patriarchy."
—Karla J. Strand, *Ms.*

"The magic within the text of Witches exists in language . . . Lozano's interest in the fluidity of a piece of art mirrors *Witches'* own interest in fluidity—of gender, time, and even the perception of reality . . . In her *Loop*, an unnamed diarist explores the awful reality of gender-based violence, but in *Witches*, Lozano uses it as a point of connection for Feliciana and Zoe. She doesn't just raise awareness of the problem but imagines a way to save lives that exists outside of oppressive structures."   —Shelbi Polk, *Shondaland*

"Who needs a standard plot when you can write as exquisitely as Brenda Lozano? . . . The women reveal themselves, through stories of mothers, daughters, sisters, lovers—men are essential but peripheral, often dangerous—in a rhythm that enchants and floats the story forward, confirming the capacity of words to cast a powerful spell."   —Cat Auer, *The A.V. Club*

"A terrific read from a writer who explores the power of the feminine in a world set on narrowly defining and belittling it."
                    —Sarah Neilson, A *them* Best Book of Summer

"Readers of Fernanda Melchor's form-busting, psychedelic takes on recent South American history won't want to miss Brenda Lozano's *Witches* . . . Heather Cleary fluidly translates Lozano's spiky narrative, immersing readers in its horrors without obscuring its beauties."   —*Chicago Review of Books*

"*Witches* is a glorious novel about gender-nonconforming people who brave a hostile world to be themselves."
                    —Eileen Gonzalez, *Foreword Reviews*

MOTHERS

ALSO BY BRENDA LOZANO

Witches

Loop

MOTHERS

A Novel

BRENDA LOZANO

TRANSLATED FROM THE SPANISH
BY HEATHER CLEARY

Catapult
New York

MOTHERS

Copyright © 2025 by Brenda Lozano
Translation copyright © 2025 by Heather Cleary

First Catapult edition: 2025

ISBN: 978-1-64622-253-7

Library of Congress Control Number: TK

Jacket design and illustration by Jaya Miceli
Jacket image of dress © Getty / Vac1
Book design by tracy danes

Catapult
New York, NY
books.catapult.co

Printed in the United States of America

1 3 5 7 9 10 8 6 4 2

For Michel Lipkes

perhaps it was left there one summer,
when the world was as white as a feast,
before I had learned that a dreamer
must dream like the trees, be a dreamer
of fruit to the last.

INGER CHRISTENSEN,
Alphabet, tr. Susanna Nied

Just as Jacob slept and Judith slept, Boaz lay there
Underneath a bed of leaves and gently closed his eyes.
For when the gate of heaven opened over his head
A dream went out and drifted downwards through the skies.

And in this dream Boaz saw an oak tree grow out of
The middle of his stomach and ascend into the blue.
A nation climbed upward like the links of a chain:
A king sung at the bottom and a God died above.

VICTOR HUGO,
"Boaz Asleep," tr. Steven Monte

The sea
smiles from far off.
Teeth of foam,
lips of sky.

FEDERICO GARCÍA LORCA,
"The Seawater Ballad," tr. Scott Horton

PART ONE

We hear this is what happened:

1.

THE RAIN WOKE HER THAT NIGHT. GLORIA FELIPE, who could be stirred by the slightest noise, managed a few more hours of sleep. It was still dark the next time she awoke, and still raining over the vast, sleeping city, but it slowed to a drizzle and stopped entirely before daybreak. The January sun was no match for the wind blowing winter's cold down the almost empty avenue on the other side of her window. The bad feeling that stirred in her, like all bad things, had only one possible interpretation.

On the morning of January 22, 1946, Gloria Felipe left the house wearing a pale blue dress with a matching bolero jacket and a navy hat; she carried a white purse under one arm and with the other held the hand of her daughter, the only one of her five children still too young to attend school. Little Gloria Miranda Felipe had turned two just three weeks earlier and that morning had gone with her mother to drop her siblings off in a new white dress with yellow flowers embroidered on the chest, made especially for her by her grandmother Ana María as a birthday gift. Gloria Felipe thought the dress was too elegant for everyday wear, but the little girl had refused to leave the house in anything else and Consuelo had given in. They had just reached one of the iron gates to the building's courtyard when they ran into Hortensia, a

3

young girl new to the block who enjoyed playing with the neighbors' children.

The Miranda Felipe family lived on the second floor of La Mascota, a French-style building on Calle Bucareli in Colonia Juárez. Gustavo Miranda kept his moustache neatly trimmed and always wore a suit and a hat, like his colleagues at the national telephone company. Mrs. Gloria Felipe, who was in charge of the household, had worked for her mother, Ana María Felipe, at the beauty salon and in the atelier where her mother designed evening and wedding gowns; she even helped with the administration of a few of her mother's properties. Which is to say that she worked, only without pay. The couple lived in a large apartment in La Mascota with their five children and Consuelo, the domestic worker—who back then would have been called a maid. Their firstborn, Gustavo, was twelve years old and had a large, heart-shaped birthmark on his right hand that he was teased about at the all-boys school he attended, and which he had poked a few times with a drawing compass in the hope of distorting its form; he was loyal to his brothers and liked to give them a hard time, though his siblings were the center of his world. To Ana María Felipe's great chagrin, her first grandson was the one who most resembled the Spaniard whose name we will not speak, Gloria Felipe's father. They sometimes called him Tavo, to differentiate him from his father. Luis, at eleven years old, was the skinniest of the five and liked to read, which was unusual in a house with so few books; he was the most introverted and enjoyed standing under an umbrella on rainy days. Jesús, who was nine, looked most like his father. As a matter of fact, the family had a pair of photographs that seemed like an image and its copy but were actually pictures of the father and son as young boys. Jesús even made the same facial expressions as his father and, in an attempt to gain still more of his approval, he dreamed of working for Teléfonos de México like him. Carlos was five and had just learned to read; trying to emulate his older brothers, he liked to play with his new words, even though he used many of them like he was blindfolded in a game of pin-the-tail-on-the-donkey. Gloria, the youngest, was the only person in the world identical to Ana María Felipe: she had honey-colored eyes, thick lashes and brows, beautiful features, and freckles scattered across her arms and back. Gustavo, who invented nicknames to annoy all his siblings, sometimes called her "chile-dusted jicama." Gloria was just learning her first words; she put simple sentences together as if she were piling wooden blocks on top of one another, and the pile often came crashing down.

Consuelo had arrived with few belongings at the Miranda Felipe residence from Tlalpujahua de Rayón, Michoacán, at the age of twenty-four. She moved into the servant's quarters in less than half an hour and began to work like day breaks and night falls. She had a daughter named Alicia, who was being looked after by her grandparents. Consuelo had arrived a few weeks before Luis was born and since then had prayed every night with the same rosary she'd had in her hands when Gustavo and Gloria came home with him in their arms. Her face spoke volumes; she couldn't lie, and it never crossed her mind to do so. At thirty-five years old, she looked either twenty-five or forty-five, and that was the only ambiguity about her. She loved to sing rancheras and braided her long hair into a thick plait every day while it was still wet. No one ever saw her wavy locks at the end of the day, since she never let her hair down in front of anyone but Jesus Christ, who hung on the wall beside her bed and to whom she prayed every night. In her mind, he was a living presence in the room, and she felt comfortable with her hair loose in front of him, as if he were her husband, someone who knew her in her most private moments.

While we're on the subject of introductions, I should proba-bly present myself. I wouldn't want you thinking I was some male omniscient narrator. I'm not a third-person know-it-all who con-trols the story, the voice of a white male saying this is like this and that is like that and these characters are going to say blah-blah or blah-blah-blah when I want them to because I'm in control of the vertical and the horizontal. Not at all. I'm not some abstract voice, either—I have a body. I'm a woman, and also a third-person narrator. This is my job. You'll lose sight of me sometimes, but I'll still be here. I'll step aside and listen when someone else speaks, and when all this mischief is over, I'll just say THE END instead of slopping more crema on the taco. Oh, and don't think I'm some generic woman, either: I'm Mexican, which means my words dance the jarabe tapatío; don't expect me to talk like a Miami anchorwoman. You've probably already noticed that I like to dip my spoon in the story, but you might not know that, like Con-suelo, I also know my way around a ranchera. Now that all that's out of the way, let's get down to business.

Gloria Felipe opened the heavy iron gate to the building's courtyard and leaned against it while her daughter said something to Hortensia, who asked Gloria if they could play. Little Glo-ria stretched her hands toward the older girl before her mother even gave permission. Seeing this, Gloria told Hortensia to stay in the courtyard, where she could keep an eye on them. They could play for a little while, but Gloria needed to go to the market soon and, she added unnecessarily, bring her mother some documents at the shop. As her daughter squealed and clapped at the sight of Hortensia taking a piece of chalk from one of the large pockets on her dress and drawing the first box for a game of hopscotch, Glo-ria Felipe thought she could use the time to do a few things before going out again. Though Hortensia seemed to enjoy herself during these games, too, her patience with younger children inspired confidence. Gloria thought she was the daughter of the doorman across Bucareli, a widower, but she had never asked.

Gloria Felipe was inside her home for sixteen minutes. She used the bathroom and checked what was left in the pantry, the refrigerator, and the kitchen baskets to make her shopping list. Consuelo was washing dishes. Gloria began to tidy a few things her children had left lying around but did not finish the task, thinking that she shouldn't leave her daughter outside any longer, and besides it was time she got moving and maybe she ought to see her mother first, so she grabbed a small but heavy blue wool peacoat that Ana María had made for her only granddaughter, with its big golden anchor buttons and rounded collar flaps, and hurried down the stairs. She was certain her mother would approve of her granddaughter's outfit.

When she opened the door to the courtyard, Gloria Felipe saw a little airplane drawn on the ground and two stones on different numbers of the hopscotch court. Fear swelled in her. She looked in every direction and the fear sharpened. A cry broke free and she shouted her daughter's name, which was her own. She shouted her daughter's name, her own name, as if by losing her daughter she had somehow lost herself. Thinking that perhaps the girls had gone to the shop a few blocks away, she set off in that direction, shouting her daughter's name as she crossed the avenue. Despite her hope that she would find them there, Gloria Felipe had a bad feeling, which resembled the one that had unsettled her in the middle of the night or was the very same one. The widower doorman poked his head out like a mole from its burrow, and when Gloria Felipe asked him if her daughter was with his, as if pulling a line taut, he replied that he had only one daughter, who was grown and married now, and Gloria felt a bolt of lightning run through her body, announcing the storm to come, and like the thunder that follows lightning, she screamed her daughter's name. But who was supposed to hear her? Her daughter didn't seem to be listening; she didn't even seem to be nearby. To whom was she shouting her own name? To herself, or to her daughter?

A man approached her, trying to help, but Gloria couldn't speak and pushed him aside. He was wasting her time; in fact, everything that didn't bring her closer to her daughter was wasting her time. But was she getting closer to her daughter? Was she getting closer, or was she moving farther away? How could she know if she was closer or farther? How could she know? Gloria crossed the avenue again, ignoring traffic, and someone swerved to avoid running her over. She managed to knock on the door of Josefina López, the building administrator who lived on the first floor and knew after taking one look at Gloria that something was terribly wrong.

"Hortensia took Gloria," she managed to say. It was like trying to hold water in her hands.

Josefina told her that the girls had probably just gone off to buy sweets. Without answering, Gloria rushed up to the second floor, taking the steps two at a time, and opened the door to her apartment, moving as she had never done before: wracked with doubt, with fear. She acted like someone who suddenly finds they've been cast as the protagonist of a tragedy, but she didn't want to act, she didn't know how, she had no interest in acting in a tragedy, much less in a tragedy that was her own life. And yet, there she was, stepping onstage, opening the door to her home in desperation, not knowing what would happen in the next minute, moving like the tragic protagonist she now realized she was. This was her only certainty because it was about her daughter who had been taken; now it was clear that her sense of foreboding that morning had been right, that her bad feeling had been right and now it and her reality were like the sea's fury and the wind pounding against one another, recognizing themselves in one another. The distance from the front door to the telephone had never seemed so vast as when she tried to cross it to call the police, because it would be better if they, if not only she and her husband and mother, were looking for her daughter. She wanted, she desperately needed, more characters on this stage.

My daughter was kidnapped, sir, said Gloria, struggling not to cry as she named what she had not wanted to name before that moment but named now because she needed to know that the person on the other end of the line understood, really understood, what had just happened. Captain Rubén Darío Hernández, head of Special Operations, better known around police headquarters as Two Poems, had just begun his shift and was enjoying his breakfast of an egg sandwich and sweetened atole, which he was drinking from a mug that he set on his desk when the phone rang.

"Where was your daughter kidnapped, ma'am?"

"She was taken from outside my home, on the corner of Bucareli and Cuauhtémoc in Colonia Juárez. She was right there, outside."

"Did you see the person or persons who took her?"

"No, I left her playing with another little girl."

"How old is your daughter, ma'am?" Captain Rubén Darío asked her serenely, setting his egg sandwich down beside his typewriter and cradling the receiver between his shoulder and his ear to take notes.

Gloria Felipe gave him her daughter's date of birth and the exact time escaped her lips, too, as if that detail marked the girl cosmically as her daughter, and only hers, as if God could hear her speak with such precision, as if that were the key to bringing

9

a daughter back to her mother, knowing the exact hour and minute when she came into this world before dawn two years and three weeks earlier, a detail only she knew because Gustavo, not wanting the boys to spend a night without him in the house, had not gone to the hospital with her, a fact she complained about and would continue to make passive aggressive comments about whenever the opportunity arose. He had chosen to be with his four sons rather than with her, his wife, as she gave birth, yes, her fifth birth; he had left her there just before she split open and began to bleed, she had been the only one to feel that pain in her body, and as if one pain were being piled on top of another, Gloria sobbed as she answered the questions that followed. Captain Rubén Darío tried to calm her with clichés. He needed more information. He asked for the minor's full name and asked Gloria to bring photographs of the girl down to headquarters in order to open a case file.

After hanging up with Gloria Felipe, Captain Rubén Darío Hernández of Special Operations wrote on his typewriter: "Mexico City, January 22, 1946. Report: kidnapping of Gloria Miranda Felipe, born December 30, 1943 (at 1:34am!!)"

Mrs. Gloria Felipe called her husband at the national telephone company and then called her mother, who was at the atelier, attending to a film and theater actress who required a dress for a party. Beatriz, Ana María's assistant, was calling to her with one hand over the receiver when Josefina knocked on the door to tell Gloria that she had gone to the corner store and had asked around the building if anyone had seen the girl, and that Consuelo was out in the street looking, too. Gloria closed the door without saying a word and returned to the phone, where her mother waited on the other end of the line.

The country was plagued by a wave of kidnappings. In 1946,

Mexico City had a population of two million, and just four thousand police officers—as grossly underpaid then as they are today—who divided their labor in three shifts. Special Operations was the only state organ that worked kidnappings; Captain Rubén Darío Hernández had investigated several such cases, some of which had been solved while others remained open. Since the police were overrun, the Charitable Organization Against the Theft of Infants was formed in response to a group of parents searching for their children. It was, however, a new organization and had fewer resources than the police. On January 22 of that year, Special Operations had eleven cases open, children ranging in age from three months to five years, while the COATI had fifty-four; the file they opened on Gloria Miranda Felipe was their twelfth. In those days, the media offered two main hypotheses to explain the rampant abduction of minors: the missing children were either being sold to families abroad or they were being forced to beg in the streets of the rapidly growing city by vagrants or immigrants as their sole source of income.

Ana María Felipe had removed her ex-husband's name from her only daughter's birth certificate and had registered her as an "extramarital birth" after divorcing him when Gloria Felipe was five years old. Gloria's father, whose name Ana María refused to speak, so we will do the same, was a Spanish refugee with blue eyes and many words, a torrent of words he couldn't control when he drank, as if he were a burst pipe. His voice made an impression wherever he went. He had an explosive laugh like that moment when a plate breaks in a restaurant and everyone turns around, and he spoke a rapid peninsular Spanish that many people in Mexico had trouble following. He was an alcoholic, and he was violent. Ana María was five months pregnant when the Spaniard beat her and she miscarried, discovering right then that there

11

were two babies inside her rather than one. Ana María Felipe was twenty-eight years old when she lost the twins. After the miscarriage, she had a hysterectomy, a five-year-old daughter, and a mother who was, like her and her child, financially dependent on the Spaniard. She also had a suitcase, which she filled with clothes, and another little bag for the odds and ends she took before leaving.

Gloria Felipe grew up with the stigma of being the daughter of a divorced woman who, to make matters worse, worked for a living. An unthinkable combination at the time. None of her classmates from elementary or Sunday school ever invited her over. Her mother is divorced, their parents would say. She's a bad influence, they would say. Her mother works, they would say. She's not a good example for this household, they would say. God forbid she bring the misfortune of divorce upon our family, they would say. God forbid she pass immoral ideas on to the other girls. Little by little, Gloria Felipe began to feel ashamed of sharing a surname with her mother and for not knowing her father. Sometimes she used her married name, but her mother had urged her to keep her maiden name, an unusual choice for that era, and in the end, that's what she did. She had a few grainy recollections of her father, which she had remolded so many times in her memory that she transformed him into a good man and couldn't understand why her mother had deprived her of his presence. She was angry with Ana María Felipe throughout most of her adolescence. Why wasn't she allowed to use her father's surname? What even was her father's surname? Why wasn't she allowed to look for him? Why had she been denied the chance to live with both of her parents, like the other girls did? Why had the geometry of her family been broken? And why didn't she have siblings like the other girls? As a teenager, she would scream at her mother, demanding to know why she was so selfish, not realizing that she had lost siblings, the twins—a fact Ana María would reveal to her many years later in a single terse, even cryptic, utterance.

When she divorced the Spaniard whose name will not appear in these pages, Ana María knew how to sew, embroider, and cook. With these basic skills, she began to work as a seamstress in a shop that sold women's clothing and nightgowns. Over time, she distinguished herself and was promoted to the role of assistant to the designer of formal day wear. To speed up Ana María's story, which we'll return to later on: she started her own business specializing in evening and wedding gowns, and by the time Gloria and Gustavo were married, she was a famous designer and traveled the world attending runway shows, purchasing all kinds of textiles, buttons, and thread for her designs. Ana María Felipe was the first female designer in Mexico to achieve such international renown. She also owned a beauty salon that enjoyed an excellent reputation and a loyal clientele because, in addition to being a celebrated professional in the world of fashion and beauty, Ana María was tremendously charismatic. Her employees and her clients all adored her. In fact, her charisma and her professionalism were like fire and air, one fed the other, and people approached her at parties even if they didn't know her. She had a wonderful sense of humor and treated her wealthy clients no differently than the employees who depended on her. This warmth of hers generated tremendous loyalty among the women who worked for her. Ana María had a policy of hiring only women so those in situations similar to her own would have someone to turn to after running from the insults, shouts, and sometimes the fists of their former husbands. Word got around that if a woman wanted to get divorced, Ana María would find her a job. Her businesses were booming. Maybe she was like a lotus, which can grow from mud to become one of the most beautiful flowers in the world; a woman who blossomed after experiencing adversity and loss.

The apartment in Colonia Juárez was a wedding gift from Ana María to her daughter and son-in-law, and the luxuries they afforded themselves as a big family were also thanks to her. When her daughter called that morning, Ana María told her that she couldn't leave the atelier right then, but she would be on her way in just a few minutes; she'd also send her assistant, Beatriz, to pick up her four grandchildren at school so her cook could watch them. Even as an adult, Gloria was hurt that her mother didn't leave work immediately, given the situation. Time had not healed the wound of abandonment. The few times she had managed to express this, clumsily, her mother had replied that it wasn't that she cared more about work but that she cared so much about her daughter that she worked to give her everything she might need. It was one of the ways she showed love, but Gloria wanted her mother. She wanted her mother to leave work that instant and run to her side. Together with the anguish she felt at not knowing where her daughter was, it was all too much. She burst into tears like a five-year-old. Maybe because time stops there, right at the point we've been most deeply wounded.

Gustavo came home. He almost always wore a pin with the Teléfonos de México logo on his lapel, not because it was mandatory, but rather out of gratitude to the organization that had hired him as a telegraph operator at the age of sixteen. His wife, who sat weeping on the toilet, blamed herself for leaving their daughter alone. How could I have trusted Hortensia with her? she managed to whimper, her nose running into her mouth. Who's Hortensia? Gustavo asked, as he cleaned his wife's face with toilet paper. Flagellating herself with every word, she answered: I'm an idiot, an imbecile, I thought she was our neighbor, I thought she was the daughter of the doorman across the street. Gustavo leaned her against the toilet, stood, and brought his hands to his hips, then he joined his hands behind his back, released them, brought them to his ribs, and scratched one shoulder where he had an itch, as if he didn't know what to do with his body, where to put it, what to do with his long and useless arms; his hands seemed extraneous, extremities that could do nothing to remedy the situation, so what did he need them for? He looked at the clock. His sons would be in school for another three hours before Beatriz went to collect them and bring them to Ana María's house. He dialed the school to let them know who would be picking up his sons. With one hand, he played with the pencil they kept beside their rotary telephone—to put those ridiculous hands to some use, at least—and as he hung up with the other hand and waited for the tone before dialing the number of Special Operations with the back of the pencil, he asked his wife the name of the officer who had helped her. "Like the poet?" he asked.

Captain Rubén Darío Hernández asked Mr. Miranda to bring a few photographs of his daughter to headquarters as soon as possible. Gustavo went to the closet in their bedroom where they kept linens and removed three pictures from the family photo albums stored in a trunk: one from when little Gloria was a baby, and two of her with the cake at her recent birthday party. Then he went into the bathroom to coax his wife to her feet; without her sweater and purse, she stepped into the street on her husband's arm. Consuelo, who was just on her way back, crossed herself and clasped Gloria's hand once she saw the look in her eyes. The couple got into a taxi and rode silently in the back seat, holding their emotions back with reason, as if rational thoughts were or could be a dam, while the taxi driver told them how he had gotten out of a traffic jam caused by an accident, a young man selling fresh rolls from his bicycle had been run over by a streetcar. He mentioned the bread scattered across the pavement, and as Gloria pictured the white rolls against the black pavement, white spots against a black expanse, a starry abyss, she was reminded how small she was, how little control she had. Even worse than the knowledge she couldn't control the situation was the fact that she couldn't control herself. Looking out the window, she thought about all the dangers her little girl was exposed to now, like the young man with his rolls, and burst into tears. It seemed there was nowhere to hide from worst-case scenarios.

At the far end of the first floor of the precinct, in a strikingly narrow office with an enormous oak desk that held a heavy black typewriter and a few documents in apparent disorder, Captain Rubén Darío Hernández chose one of the girl's photographs and shouted to a young policeman named Octavio, who had a crew cut, a cleft lip, and rigorously polished boots, that this was the photograph they would send to police headquarters all over the country and to the authorities in the United States. Octavio left the office, and Rubén Darío stared at the remaining photograph, which was identical to the other except for the smile. He was certain that the press would love the image of a little girl smiling in front of her birthday cake, with her parents standing behind her, and suggested that the newspapers use it to get the word out. It was, in part, for this kind of sensitivity that he was known around headquarters as Two Poems.

Gustavo asked permission to sit beside his wife, and from that perspective was able to see the food stains on Rubén Darío's shirt, right where his belly bulged. It was for this kind of thing that the captain was also known as Two Tacos, but around headquarters they usually called him Two Poems. Mr. Miranda told him that his wife had left their daughter playing with Hortensia in the courtyard of La Mascota, and even on the sidewalk on Calle Bucareli, on several prior occasions without any issue. Captain Rubén Darío Hernández took notes and asked Mrs. Felipe to describe in detail Hortensia's appearance, how she had come to meet the girl, and what had occurred that morning. Meanwhile, Mr. Miranda read the names of the other kidnapped children from the papers on the desk and, when the interview with the captain had ended, he suggested to Gloria that they leave a copy of their daughter's photograph with the two biggest radio stations and the newspaper with the largest circulation. Rubén Darío suggested a newspaper and even offered the name of a reporter, but they did not seem to hear him.

Gloria Felipe asked her husband to call her mother first. Ana María was already at her daughter's apartment with Consuelo, and she got them an appointment with the director of the newspaper with the highest circulation. Following his supervisor's orders, though Rubén Darío had already brought the case to his attention, the reporter José Córdova asked the couple a few questions and took the photograph of their daughter. The text that appeared under the picture in the evening edition, which broke the news, read: "Do you know the whereabouts of Gloria Miranda Felipe? The little girl, who recently turned two, was last seen today at 8:20 a.m. on the corner of Bucareli and Cuauhtémoc, in Colonia Juárez; her current whereabouts are unknown. At the time of her disappearance, Gloria Miranda Felipe was wearing a white dress embroidered across the chest with dark yellow flowers, brown leather shoes with buckles and three leaf-shaped perforations, white stockings, and a ribbon tying her hair back in a half ponytail. Description: slim build, brown hair, delicate features, thick eyebrows and lashes, small mouth and plump lips. She knows a few words and is allergic to milk, which gives her a rash on her chest and forearms. Her parents would be grateful for information and offer a 15,000-peso reward to whomever might be able to provide such. Please contact the girl's father, Mr. Gustavo Miranda, at the following telephone number."

Gloria Felipe stared at the front page of the freshly printed newspaper as if she were watching a ship cast off in the middle of the night. And she felt the sea inside her.

2

THE LITTLE GIRL'S CASE BECAME A TOPIC OF CONVER-
sation on the street and in offices and homes. Thanks to their
privilege, the Miranda Felipe family had been able to get special
treatment from the police and space on the front page of the biggest newspaper in the country. If their case was being discussed on
a national level, why wasn't the same thing happening for all the
other kidnapped children? The waters were stagnant on one side
and rushing on the other. Gloria Miranda Felipe's case sparked ex-
changes about the wave of kidnappings on the radio. Word spread
on public transportation and in upper-middle-class households.
How could this have happened to one of their own? There was talk
of gangs from Tepito, from Japan, from South America; there was
talk of criminal networks selling Mexican children in the United
States and Europe after World War II. There was even speculation
that some of those children were being sold in the North so mil-
itary widows could claim bigger pensions. In those days, racism,
classism, and xenophobia grew in the streets like grass pushing
through cracks in the pavement. All it took was a mother and her
child passing someone with darker skin, "an oriental" or a "gypsy,"
to unleash all sorts of violent speech.

It was a hot topic, even more so because the killing of a minor had been all over the news that week. A man had taken the life of a four-year-old boy in broad daylight, right in front of a café on Calle Tacuba. The guilty party said that he had meant to rob the child's mother and that the death had been an accident. The Kiddie Killer, as one headline called him—and the name spread like wildfire—was in Lecumberri Prison, known also at the time as the Black Palace. The court's verdict clarified that the Kiddie Killer's intention had not been to rob the child's mother but rather to murder the child, and that he was also guilty of murdering five other children, whom he buried in his garden.

Nuria Valencia had heard about the case a few days earlier on the radio she shared with Constanza, her coworker at a cardiologist's office in Mexico's General Hospital. Nuria, who had a young daughter, wondered what pleasure a killer might derive from murder. And, even worse, what pleasure a child killer might derive from the act. How could it be possible to kill a child and feel some kind of pleasure?

Nuria Valencia learned of Gloria Miranda Felipe's kidnapping while listening to the radio in her kitchen. In the time it took to pour herself a glass of water, she decided that no information about the case would enter her house where she lived with her daughter, husband, and parents, so she locked the radio away in a sideboard in the living room. The little girl was already quite sheltered, and hiding the radio seemed a bit extreme to Nuria's father, Gonzalo Valencia, but he had seen his daughter make decisions based on fear before and he understood her perspective.

Nuria Valencia had been trying for years to get pregnant with her husband, Martín Fernández Mendía, who was slightly older than her. Before their daughter Agustina arrived, they had fought often. Once, Martín even threatened to leave her if she didn't get pregnant. He longed to be a father; he wanted a family and was tired of waiting. Agustina Mendía, Martín's mother, had been in-sinuating for years that he should leave Nuria, though that would have been the case whether or not they'd started a family years earlier; it also would have been the case no matter whom Martín had chosen as his wife. Nuria Valencia Pérez had visited several gynecologists and one endocrinologist in recent years, when her need to get pregnant grew ever more pressing. It was a sensitive topic for the couple, more so as time wore on. Both wanted to be parents, but it simply wasn't happening. Each of these doctors, all of whom were men over the age of fifty, said she was sterile, until one of them, using an innovative technique, diagnosed her with an obstruction of the Fallopian tubes that impeded the movement of her eggs and proposed a treatment that involved filling her uterus with gases to unblock her tubes, at which point her eggs would be freed from her ovaries, ready to be fertilized.

Nuria Valencia went to five sessions of this gas therapy. The doctor had prepared a calendar of the dates Nuria and Martín should try to get pregnant, and she followed the schedule to the letter, even if neither of them had any desire to sleep together. The first time she received the treatment, she let out several yelps and got so dizzy from the pain that she nearly fainted. The second time, she vomited in the bathroom of the doctor's office. The third time, she did faint. The fourth time, too. Her husband had to get her; he had been in a meeting in the offices of the movie theater where he worked when a nurse called to say that they had been unable to finish the procedure because his wife had lost consciousness. The fifth time, Nuria took several painkillers before leaving work and afterward had a migraine that stayed with her until the following night. The sixth time, having seen no results despite the extreme pain she had come to know so well, she gave up on the treatment and, without telling her husband, took a taxi from the clinic to the orphanage she had seen on her way to the hospital where she worked. She was going to fill out the paperwork necessary to begin the adoption process.

Mexico is famous for its lines and bureaucracy. It always has been. The paperwork required for an adoption, like so many other processes, was a labyrinth with no apparent way in or out; it wasn't even clear there was a minotaur at its center. After a few more cycles during which she didn't get pregnant, Nuria had a talk with Martín. She proposed that they consider adopting and, contrary to her expectations, he was open to the idea. He told her, sincerely, that he was willing to forgo having a firstborn who looked like him and added, for the first time since that terrible fight, that he wanted to make a family with her. But if we're going to adopt, he said, we're adopting a boy so we can name him Martín Fernández, just like me. Nuria found it strange that this was her husband's first concern, given that the other person with that name, his father, had abandoned him and his mother. Especially knowing that there already *was* another Martín Fernández, beside him and his father: the son of the woman he'd left Martín's mother for. He'd named the boy after himself as if he were trading in his firstborn for this other child. The child who *had* grown up with a father. Why was her husband's first paternal impulse so much like his father's?

Adopting a newborn was a complex process in which the applicants had no say over the child's biological gender. Martín left the bureaucracy to Nuria. They would talk at night about how things were going, and after a period of waiting they couldn't characterize as long or short, they managed to adopt not a little boy, as Martín had wished, but a little girl—their daughter, Agustina Fernández Valencia. Martín had suggested that, while they sorted out the paperwork, Nuria could fake a pregnancy with a pillow so their friends would think the baby was biologically theirs. Not only did this idea not make much sense, but the date of the adoption was moved up so Martín abandoned the idea and instead proposed, or rather imposed, that they name the girl after his mother.

3

THE PHONE AT THE MIRANDA FELIPE RESIDENCE HAD
been ringing off the hook. Because Consuelo couldn't read or
write, Ana María asked Beatriz to help her take down messages
while they were out. Beatriz took notes on a little pad. Most were
women calling to offer words of support to the family. One older
lady, who seemed out of breath from the effort of speaking, told
Beatriz that if the Miranda Felipe household needed, she could
send them meals from her restaurant every day until the girl was
found. Beatriz wrote everything down, including phone numbers
in case Gustavo or Gloria wanted to return any of the calls. At
one point, she needed to go to the store for a moment and was just
closing the apartment door when the phone rang. She hurried back
inside, but the caller had hung up after the second ring. While she
was gone, Consuelo repeated the Lord's Prayer on her knees in
front of the telephone with her eyes closed and her hands clasped.
When she returned, Beatriz heard the phone ringing through the
door again and felt guilty for lingering with the building's administrator, who had asked her a few questions and told her that
the family's neighbor was taking her children and moving out of
the building. She heard the phone ringing and would never have
forgiven herself if she had been too late to pick up. Beatriz held

the receiver to her ear and a man's voice—a voice that slid hoarsely over the end of each word like coal, smudging its passage—said, "The girl's alive, but if you want to keep her that way, be at the Monument to the Revolution at seven o'clock tonight. You'll give me the money, and I'll give you an address where you can find the girl. You'll recognize me because I'll be wearing one black glove. Then you'll wait twenty-four hours before going to the address so I can get out of the city, but that's where you'll find the girl." And he hung up.

Beatriz's heart raced as she took down the message. When the phone in her hand gave off a dial tone, she felt one of her eyelids begin to twitch and thought she was about to faint, but she had managed to transcribe each of the man's stained, rumpled words. She had plummeted into the abyss this way three times in her life. The first, at the technical school where she had studied typing. She began to feel as if she might die right there in the hall-way; her heart seemed like it wanted to burst straight through her chest; she ended up in the infirmary begging for an ambulance, but they managed to slow her respiration with just a paper bag. The second time was when she sensed that her boyfriend, her first love, was being unfaithful to her. She went to his house without warning and confirmed her suspicion: he opened the door in socks, and she caught a glimpse of a girl with no shoes on in the living room. She started feeling ill on her way home; her eyelid began to twitch, warning her that what came next was the racing heart and then the hyperventilation, and then maybe death, so she bought a newspaper from some boy standing on a corner, improvised a paper bag, and managed to calm herself down. The third time was in Ana María's store, trapped in a fitting room with an espe-cially cruel client. Those were her first panic attacks, which were probably known by other names back then. She felt another one building inside her just as the phone rang again. She desperately needed a paper bag. Consuelo helped her look to see if there was a bag somewhere from a loaf of bread; Beatriz was in no condition to answer the phone, which kept ringing even though she needed a paper bag before she could talk to that man or anyone else, for that matter. She found a magazine in a drawer in the kitchen, tore out a page to make a bag, and shut herself in a bathroom until she was able to control her respiration. Consuelo was waiting for her on the other side of the door, telling her that she was there if Beatriz needed anything. When her hands stopped shaking and her eyelid and entire body slipped out of the spotlight, Beatriz called Ana María, who would get the ransom money together. Ana María, as calm as a doctor in the midst of a crisis, dictated a message for her daughter and son-in-law, then brought the money personally to Captain Rubén Darío Hernández, with whom she reached an agreement.

Right there in the offices of Special Operations, Rubén Darío got the idea, as he snacked on peanuts he shelled between his teeth, that some of the money Ana María had brought would be replaced with newspaper clippings and scrap paper. Octavio, the police officer with a crew cut, a cleft lip, and rigorously polished boots, celebrated Rubén Darío's plan with a whistle that showed his dimples and involved sticking two fingers in his mouth. He told Ana María Felipe that it was for ideas like this one his superior was called Two Poems around headquarters. Captain Rubén Darío Hernández opened the cloth bag with the "ransom," and Ana María was surprised by how real it looked; just then, her daughter walked in with Ignacio Rodríguez Guardiola and they left with the bag.

Gloria Felipe went to the Monument to the Revolution escorted by a young agent from Special Operations named Ignacio

Rodríguez Guardiola, who at twenty-two years of age found joy in three things: soccer, anything related to soccer, and—sometimes—his mother's chilaquiles. They didn't see a man with a single black glove anywhere near the meeting point.

Gloria Felipe was nervous. Rodríguez Guardiola was dressed as a civilian, the bag was a bag, and the money seemed to all be there, but she was acutely conscious of her own movements. She was afraid that the unnatural way she was moving, and not the fake money, would make her seem suspicious. A year earlier, her son Jesús had told her that he'd realized something important when his father had taken him and his brothers swimming: when he peed in the pool and then kicked hard to make the yellow stain in the water disappear, his plan worked against him—the more he moved around to hide what he'd done, the more obvious it was to everyone that he had just peed in the water. Why did she feel like her son right then, peeing in a pool the size of her entire life? She felt as if the way she was moving could sabotage the thing she most wanted. And what guarantee did she have that the one-gloved man's story wasn't as fake as the money she was carrying? This feeling hit her like a wave of heat, like an image, a sensation, an intuition just as she was moving strangely in front of the Monument to the Revolution; if she could have, she would have peed in her clothes right there in the middle of that public space, but instead she burst into tears. A man who had been walking toward her paused and then suddenly started running in the opposite direction. Gloria watched him go and sank to her knees, weeping; Rodríguez Guardiola, who looked like a teenager in civilian clothes, maybe even like Gloria's son, helped her to her feet, and they walked back to the car together. Had they scared off the kidnapper? That man who had run off, was he the one who had taken her daughter? Gloria was certain she'd made a mess

28

of things when it mattered most. She knew the kidnapper was walking toward her, she knew she was carrying a fake ransom, she knew that she was supposed to be there alone and she had made a terrible mistake. She had scared off the man who was going to give her daughter back. How could she ever forgive herself?

At eleven o'clock that night, after Gustavo had put his four sons to bed—he was usually the one who did this because he enjoyed reading them stories and generally enjoyed being a father, a fact he readily acknowledged, despite the trouble he usually had communicating his emotions—the phone rang, and he grabbed the receiver.

"Hello?"

The voice on the other end of the line sounded like the one Beatriz had described to Ana María.

"It's important that you follow my instructions." These last three, almost unintelligible words were pronounced like one, as if instead of words, the man were speaking in stains. "I'll give you another chance. Your wife should go alone; no one should be with her. Do you understand me?"

"Do you swear not to hurt my wife or my daughter?"

"Your daughter is alive and she'll stay that way as long as you follow my instructions. Do you understand me, Mr. Miranda?"

"Go on."

"In Colonia Escandón, on José Martí just off Sindicalismo, there's a little mom-and-pop restaurant. I'll be there tomorrow, at seven in the evening, with my back to the door and a newspaper covering my face. In exchange for the money, I'll give your wife the address where you'll find your daughter. Wait twenty-four hours before going to get her so I have time to leave the city."

Guilt was a familiar sensation for Gloria, but now, in the freefall of insomnia, she thought about how it would be doubly

29

her fault if anything were to happen to her daughter. The vertigo of losing her twice. The man's phone call had sent her into the darkest reaches of the place inside her where guilt, perhaps the coldest feeling, resided. Gloria couldn't fall asleep that night; questions formed a circle around her, hounding her until she could hardly breathe. She felt anxious, tight in the chest. Gustavo was fast asleep.

Something strange happened that night. Her husband said something she couldn't understand. She realized that he was talking in his sleep and thought he might reveal how he felt about the situation, since he hadn't said a word and she wanted to know, but instead he started talking about a coffee plantation. Look at the coffee, at those plants over there, thank you, thank you, said Gustavo to no one at all. After that came a phrase that was more like an incomprehensible whisper, followed by a list of numbers in no discernable order. The number eleven made her husband laugh. What was so funny about that number? Maybe it was an encrypted message, some secret language he was using to express his feelings. She had no memory of their ever traveling together to a coffee plantation, not before their wedding or after, and no idea what those random numbers might mean, much less why eleven seemed so funny to him, but she set aside her speculations and the guilt soon returned.

Who was that man? Why had he kidnapped her daughter? Why had he run in the opposite direction? Why wasn't he wearing a black glove, like he said he would? Wasn't the detail about the one glove ridiculous enough to believe what he said? Should she go to the restaurant without Rodríguez Guardiola? What if his presence had compromised her daughter's rescue again? Should she bring all the money? And what if she made a mistake? If she lost control again, might she make an even bigger mistake? A worse mistake? Might she do something else that put distance between her and her daughter, rather than bringing her closer? What if she was compromising her daughter's rescue?

In the spiral of her insomnia, Gloria remembered the time she chided her daughter for eating a bowl of strawberries meant for the whole family. Consuelo had given her the bowl and Gloria had blamed the little girl. The memory tormented her because her reaction had been so disproportionate. The strawberries had made her daughter happy, and that simple pleasure rushed back to Gloria in the form of remorse, as if the combination of distance and the blinding light of her guilt let something as small as a strawberry cast an enormous shadow on the wall in front of her. She had no idea how she was going to get out of this spiral, how she was going to fall asleep, but she did resolve to ask Rodríguez Guardiola to go with her to the restaurant, though to please stay one block away. If there was any hope of saving her daughter, it was by following the kidnapper's orders. She didn't care if the police caught the man with one glove; she cared only about getting her daughter back.

And so, the next day she got out of the car alone. To her surprise, however, there was no one in the restaurant reading a newspaper. She ordered a coffee and sat at the counter, then ordered a concha that she ate in a few bites with her coffee, not because she was hungry, but because she was acting; she wanted to act normal while she kept an eye on the door. There were just three families and one waitress in the little restaurant, and that seemed to be the entire cast of this play without an audience in which nothing happened and everyone on stage seemed bored. When asked, the waitress told her that no one had come in and read the newspaper that day. Gloria left with more questions than answers. This had officially been the first of a string of telephone calls from fake kidnappers, most of which they identified as frauds early on. Until the call they received a week later.

A woman's thick voice announced that the little girl had been taken to the Cruz Verde, and that she was probably very ill. Gloria made a few calls and determined that there were no little girls matching her daughter's description at the Cruz Verde. Another time, a teenager with a northern accent, or perhaps it was a woman who spoke like a child, told her that she'd seen Gloria Miranda Felipe cross the border holding hands with a man in a black three-piece suit and a hat who carried a brown briefcase. But what was she supposed to do with all the information and descriptions she was accumulating? All these tips, were they moving her closer to her daughter, or farther away? Was she going up or down the stairs? And her daughter, was she at the top of the staircase, or the bottom? For that matter, where was she?

Gloria Felipe knew how to swim. She had never been one for exercise, but Ana María Felipe saw swimming lessons as a kind of life insurance for her only child, so Gloria dutifully attended her lessons until she was twelve, right after her first period. Around a year after Gustavo was born, she went for a swim in the ocean. They had gone to the beach with Ana María, who wanted to buy a house there, and Gloria thought it might be nice to take a dip, but a current pulled her away from the shore and the harder she swam straight toward it, the farther away she found herself. That was how she felt: swimming straight ahead and getting farther by the day from her two-year-old daughter, while dreaming of giving her all the strawberries she could ever want.

Captain Rubén Darío Hernández was chewing something crunchy on the other end of the line when he told Gloria Felipe that the border authorities had no record of her daughter crossing into the United States. By then, the authorities had photographs

of all the kidnapped children who had open cases with Special
Operations. Why would the captain be eating something while he
gave Gloria this bad news? And what was he eating? Pork rinds?
Was this some cruel message about life going on with all its noises,
the sound of someone eating pork rinds with music in the background, all those mundane noises that didn't stop while something
terrible was happening? Why don't things come to a screeching
halt when we need a pause to match the gravity of our situation?
Why doesn't everything stop in the face of silent pain? Why would
this police officer be eating pork rinds on the other end of the line
while telling her that her daughter was still missing? How Gloria
wished that in the three weeks that had passed, during which she
had lost several pounds, even one of those phone calls had been
real, had offered—please God—some clue that had brought her
closer to her daughter. What she would have given to be free from
her own mistakes. She truly would have given anything to find her
little girl, to give her a warm bath, and to let her sleep in bed with
her and her husband, something she wasn't normally allowed to
do. To wake up with her daughter in her arms. To play with her.
It was usually Consuelo who played with the children, sometimes
as if she were a child, herself, but Gloria wanted to play with her
daughter, or she wanted to be able to. To take her to the park, play
whatever games the girl wanted. It was three, almost four o'clock
in the morning when it crossed her mind for the very first time
that someone might have sexually abused her daughter.

The moon was so bright in those small hours that it shone off
the buttons of her sleeping husband's pajamas. She spent the rest
of the night tossing and turning until Carlos called to her from
the bathroom he shared with his brothers to bring him some toilet
paper, please.

4.

MARTÍN TERNÁNDEZ WORRIED THAT PEOPLE MIGHT think they'd adopted Agustina because of an issue on his side of things. What if someone out there thought he had deficient or deformed sperm? Or, even worse, that he had none at all? What if a rumor went around that he suffered from erectile dysfunction? He was afraid of any kind of gossip on this subject, and different scenarios played out in his imagination. A few days after signing his daughter's adoption paperwork, he latched on to an idea and decided to repeat it whenever he had the chance: how much the girl looked like his own mother. Skipped a generation, he would say. Just like my dear mother, he told a neighbor who hadn't asked. Even her personality is like my mother's, he shoehorned into a conversation at work. Nuria couldn't understand why Martín was so ashamed about the adoption, but they had been waiting to be parents for so long that when it finally happened, the light of it was blinding. Where did all that light come from? She was happy. Home was the only place she wanted to be; she spent her entire shift at the hospital waiting to return.

They did the paperwork at the civil registry in Cuernavaca, where Nuria was born. There, in an office with their marriage

35

certificate, the adoption papers, and their own birth certificates, they finally registered their daughter.

Nuria had wanted to be a mother for so long that when Agustina finally came home with them, she had a suitcase waiting with clothes to cover a whole range of ages. A while ago, she had asked her mother, Carmela, to knit blankets for her future grandchild. Carmela had gone to her favorite notions store in Cuernavaca. Speaking with the attendant, she couldn't decide whether to buy blue or pink wool, so they decided on a combination of white and yellow. She bought the yarn with money she had been saving for a new pot, but it was obviously better to spend it on yarn for her future grandchild. How soft it felt to speculate amid a pile of yellow and white yarn, as if her thoughts were made of the same material. She bought enough skeins for two blankets and even treated herself to a booklet of complex patterns, then knit the blankets in the hope of getting the good news soon.

Back then, in the 1940s, it was common for photographers to take pictures of pedestrians walking around the historic district and then offer them for sale as souvenirs. Their first family portrait was taken a few days after Agustina's adoption, when they needed to run some errands there. The little girl had been sleeping, but Martín had insisted. How could they not bring her? And so they all went together, with the little girl asleep in her mother's arms. But Nuria insisted on covering her completely. Agustina was covered by one of the blankets that Carmela had knit when a photographer approached them to sell them a picture of their family walking along San Juan de Letrán: Martín in his suit and hat, Nuria in a dress that she really liked, actually, one that made her feel pretty, while having Agustina there all wrapped up made her feel happy. Nuria was carrying the little bundle cocooned in a blanket knit by her mother, completely covered. Her daughter.

She still couldn't believe it. Martín bought the photograph and gave the man a few extra cents as a tip. Martín liked this image of his family; it made him proud, as if you could feel their happiness just by looking at it. He had it framed and hung it in their living room.

Gonzalo Valencia and Carmela Pérez had just one daughter because their doctors had performed a hysterectomy in response to preeclampsia—a condition that would have been managed very differently today, of course. A gynecologist in Cuernavaca decided to remove Carmela's uterus after she gave birth to Nuria. The couple had wanted more children, but they resigned themselves to having only one and, over the years, showered their daughter with enough attention for the four or even five children of their dreams. If anyone had asked Carmela how many children she wanted, which no one ever did, she would have said as many as God saw fit to send her, but she would have been thinking five. Gonzalo would have wanted three, but no one ever asked him, either. Three children, just like his parents. And so, in their condition as parents who longed for more children, Gonzalo and Carmela had been overprotective with Nuria. If Nuria wanted to hang a picture, her father would drop whatever he was doing, day or night, and rush to her side with a hammer and nails. The couple shaped their life around their daughter's changing needs, though one thing that remained a constant was that they were always, always ready to drop whatever they were doing to take care of her, support her, or be at her side. Either would give Nuria the shirt right of their back without a second thought, and she grew used to this; if she needed some extra money, her father would leave his bill at the market unpaid or ask for a loan. "Coddled" and "spoiled" were two words that became buttons Martín knew he could push when they fought.

Gonzalo Valencia had a Spanish grandfather he'd never met; he was a man who was dedicated to running his hardware store, had a fresh scent to him, carried a small comb in his wallet, and always wore his hair parted to the side. Carmela was a housewife and liked to knit. They had scrimped and saved to help their daughter pay for several of Nuria's visits to the gynecologist in pursuit of that pregnancy they, too, longed for; this generosity contrasted sharply with that of Agustina Mendía, who did not dare verbalize her disdain for the whole situation but whose attitude spoke for itself. The battery of tests to which Nuria had subjected herself was not covered by the insurance provided to her as an employee of a public hospital—gynecology, like so many subjects related to women, was of little interest and therefore not covered by insurance because medicine was and continues to be focused on the male body—so she had to pay for them with money she and Martín had saved up and a little extra from Gonzalo and Carmela. Nuria never hesitated to ask her parents for help, despite the fact that she was a grown woman with a household of her own. She even made these requests as if they were obligated to help her. Or, rather, as if she as their only child were their eternal responsibility. Though perhaps if they had five children, they would still be supporting the youngest, so in a way Nuria was standing in for that nonexistent Benjamín.

Nuria had grown up in a simple two-bedroom house that—though it was just one story high and made of bricks, with a garden full of ferns and wild plants—enjoyed a splash of color from their wealthy next-door neighbors' bougainvillea, which spilled over into their yard. You might say the plant was like a brooch pinned to a cheap dress, giving it a little extra life. Something about the combination of the wild foliage's vibrant green and the delicacy of the flowers made the house lovely; Nuria expected her parents to give her an extra something, just like that bougainvillea did, to make her life lovelier whenever she asked. This might be a slight exaggeration, but there's truth to it, too. The frustration of not being able to get pregnant even after seeing respected doctors in the field set her at odds with her own body. And also with her understanding of life up to that point: this was the first time Nuria Valencia wasn't getting what she wanted.

Why wasn't it up to her? Why couldn't she control the outcome of this situation? Why, even after the treatment that had caused her more pain than she had ever felt in her life, had she still not gotten her reward? Why was it so easy for so many women to get pregnant, even without wanting to, when it was impossible for her? Was she incomplete because she had no children? Was she somehow defective because she couldn't get pregnant? Was something missing in her body? Could a family consist of two people, just her and her husband? Why did she feel like something was missing? And why had Martín threatened to leave her if they didn't have a child? Now all those questions, which had seemed like they were carved in stone, were washed away like a wave washes away writing in the sand. Agustina had done that. But now that she was a part of their life, why was Martín so ashamed that Agustina, who now bore their surnames and had started calling Gonzalo and Carmela "grandpa" and "grandma," was adopted? She was their daughter, after all, wasn't she? Where did the idea come from that your children are your children only if they share your blood, and if not, you're not a real parent? And while we're on the subject—don't ask me to the party if you don't like how I get down—why is it that raising a child has two different names with such different meanings, paternity and maternity, like two doors on a public bathroom? What is so different about being a mother from being a father when it comes to raising a child? The roles

39

imposed on each parent? The fact was that Nuria had been trying to get pregnant with Martín for nine years, so when Agustina appeared, she was grateful to God and, above all, to life itself. To the simple life she lived with Martín, her parents, and her daughter, each day so much like the next that they seemed to be repeated in a hall of mirrors, hours jaded by one another. Drunk on boredom. To that life full of ordinary, routine things; that life so luckily hers.

The woman we'll call Agustina's "biological" mother had been forced to give her daughter up for adoption due to a terminal illness. She was a single mother—what can you do, that's what they're called, as if being a mother were a marital status—and had no one who could take the child in upon her imminent death. Her illness, combined with the degenerative condition that had plagued her since childhood, set her in a race against time. When the doctor in charge of her case at the clinic in Cuautla told her there was no hope, Nuria told Martín, the woman wasted no time in contacting her, an old classmate from Cuernavaca. She knew that Nuria had been trying to get pregnant and wanted to propose that she adopt her two-year-old daughter. She knew that no one would be better than Nuria and Martín to care for her little girl. This is more or less what she said to Nuria from her bed in the clinic where she died just a few days later.

After several bus trips between Cuautla, her parents' house in Cuernavaca, and Mexico City, Nuria came home one night and told Martín: "It looks like a beautiful two-year-old girl will be ours, just as soon as my friend signs the papers. Maybe by the end of this week, since her health is so delicate. We might have our little girl with us next week." She had been happy at the thought but grew even more excited when she said the words out loud. Maybe because pain is neither entirely unbearable nor eternal.

5.

GLORIA FELIPE HAD RECENTLY ANSWERED A CALL from a woman who claimed to have seen her daughter in Piedras Negras, Coahuila, in the doorway of a pharmacy facing the main square, begging for change. Consuelo stayed behind to watch the boys while Gloria and Gustavo set out for the border city, accompanied by Rodríguez Guardiola, who also spoke with the woman who had contacted Gloria. They didn't see anything the day they arrived, but someone at the pharmacy said they'd seen a little girl begging for change near the square. The description they offered was vague—it could have been any girl, even her missing daughter. Gloria Felipe wanted to stay another day, but Rodríguez Guardiola had to get back to headquarters and Gustavo couldn't take any more days off work; above all, he wanted to be with his sons. He missed them. Raising them, putting them to bed at night and talking with them, was an important part of his daily routine, which was unusual back then. It's true that he worked at the national telephone company, but he could have been employed anywhere, really, since it was only by chance that he had become a telegraph operator. The real center of his world was being a father; it was what he enjoyed most and was a large part of his personality. His wife liked this about him but had, at times, felt a pang of

41

jealousy at the attention her husband lavished on their children, not to mention the fact that her childhood had been so deeply marked by her father's absence; she occasionally felt displaced by her family in her own home. They agreed that Gloria would stay one more day and Gustavo would return home to the boys.

Gloria asked about her daughter on every corner. Gustavo Miranda went back to the city that night; Consuelo came down wearing her apron over her pajamas with her hair loose and still wavy from the braid she took out when she got into bed. It was strange to see her that way, it happened so rarely. She tied her hair up in a loose bun like a reflex of modesty to tell her employer that Mrs. Ana María had come by earlier that night and had taken the boys to her house. Gustavo went over and told his mother-in-law about the trip. Three of his sons were asleep in the room where Ana María had set up two bunkbeds for her male grandchildren—her granddaughter had her own room with a single bed—and Luis was in the kitchen with the cook and another domestic worker. They were teaching the boy how to make tamales. The three of them were packing the masa into corn husks, laughing and chatting away, and Luis was happy to see his father watching him from the doorway.

The next morning, Ana María called her client and friend, the wife of the biggest newspaper in the country, to ask that they run the article about her granddaughter again. The paper took great interest in the case; in fact, the interest of its readers was more powerful than the strings Ana María thought she was pulling. By then, José Córdova had taken over the story, so the next day local newspaper boys and girls were distributing dailies that contained a brief report with updates about the case and special emphasis on the reward, which Ana María had raised to 25,000 pesos. The waters were stirred, and people began talking about the case again.

Waves travel with the tenacity of the wind. Perhaps this is the language of wind and water. And they travel like words, so much like the words of a person searching desperately for someone, until they reach the shore. This was also how the news reached the building where Nuria Valencia and Martín Fernández lived with their radio hidden away. Everyone in the household, including Gonzalo and Carmela, was deeply distressed by the wave of kidnappings, and the update set them even more on edge. A pair of twins had recently been taken in broad daylight from the park where they were roller-skating. As was the case in many households, the Miranda Felipe case made the family nervous, especially Nuria. Agustina had only ever been outside in Nuria's arms, asleep and completely covered, and she had no intention of letting her guard down. Other families, gripped by similar fears, responded in their own ways: prohibiting, punishing, overprotecting, preventing their little ones from spending time outdoors.

As often happens with cases that draw a lot of media attention, one example reveals a problem that has been affecting hundreds more for a long time already. Why should one case be given that kind of attention over any other? You might say that it was Gloria's age that made her story so scandalous, that it was her family's money that made the newspaper article stand out, or that the girl was cute and the photo taken on her birthday was moving; you might say it was the photograph that stirred people's empathy, a scene from a birthday showing how it could happen to anyone, and that it was either this vulnerability or all these things together that had helped the story spread, but the fact is that there was nothing exceptional about the case itself, it was one among many, just like one wave is similar to another. Still, the only wave we see is the one that breaks on the shore in its fury of rushing water and white foam.

A radio announcer invited the director of a grade school to her program on topics related to the home. The women discussed the Miranda Felipe kidnapping, and the director of the school said that attendance had been down because parents were so worried. They talked about the collective fear and comments they'd both heard, one as an educator and mother of two, and the other as a broadcaster with one daughter.

The newspaper that had published the first article about the case, like a mark of authority over it, had received many calls with requests for updates and also several with false leads. The second time the media reported on the story, five weeks after Gloria Miranda Felipe was kidnapped, the editor in chief asked Córdova to begin working directly with Special Operations. José Córdova had two perfectly symmetrical moles on his cheeks, an alert gaze in his big eyes, a bushy unibrow, and pointed ears. He had started losing his hair at thirty; now he was thirty-eight with a serious demeanor, few friends, a wife named Brenda, and two children. He had worked with Captain Rubén Dario Hernández of Special Operations on several cases.

Now that Gloria had returned from Coahuila without any clues about her daughter's whereabouts, an agreement was made in the Miranda Felipe household that only Beatriz and Tavo, the eldest son, were allowed to answer the phone, and that they should write every conversation down, word for word, in a notebook.

One of those days, the phone rang at five in the evening. When Tavo picked up, the person on the other end of the line didn't say anything, they just inhaled and exhaled into the receiver, and Tavo marked down the time of the call followed by the words "Call from the Breather." The next day, he answered the phone at five in the evening and wrote, "Another call from the Breather." The next day, Tavo checked his watch at exactly five in the evening, which was precisely when the person who said nothing and only breathed into the receiver called again; after five minutes had passed, according to his watch, Tavo hung up in frustration. At five o'clock on the fourth day, he asked his mother to answer the phone that was about to ring, and Gloria Felipe begged the person on the other end of the line, who was exhaling directly into the receiver as if they wanted to amplify the sound, to say something, please, but after listening to several—too many—breaths, she hung up in frustration.

Gloria was taking medication for anxiety, depression, and insomnia, but that night she couldn't sleep at all. Even stronger than the pills was her guilt over not having been more patient on the phone. What if the person who called every day at five had important information about her daughter? What if the hour itself was a message? What did it mean that they called at that time? And how was her daughter? Was she in danger? Where the hell was she? Why the hell wasn't she at home where she belonged? When that vortex of fear arrived, when her stomach flipped over at the thought of what might be happening to her daughter in a country where children were being taken all the time and the police had neither the training nor the resources to bring them home, she went into a spiral. She got out of bed to pray to the Son of God, who was nailed to a cross in their living room. She prayed and prayed until her knees froze and she went to the kitchen for a glass of water with the ridges of the floor still pressed into her flesh. Gloria believed in God more now than she had before her daughter's kidnapping, not because she didn't believe in him before, not because she needed him more now, but because God seemed to have abandoned them entirely, making his presence all the more felt.

That night, Gloria Felipe de Miranda, thirty-five years old, with four sons asleep at home, one kidnapped daughter, and a husband who tended to snore, leaned against the doorway of the kitchen with an untouched glass of water in her hand to the sound of cars passing along Avenida Bucareli like roosters announcing the dawn and wondered who the hell had called her home four days in a row at five in the evening only to breathe into the receiver on the other end of the line. Why didn't this person say anything? Or was the nothing they said their way of saying something? And just like that, the questions closed in around her. What did nothing, or that particular nothing, mean? Was that nothing of words as vast as the nothing she felt inside?

Their telephone number was public; they had also published their address, and that morning the first doorbell to ring was theirs.

As the building administrator, Josefina was usually aware of who was entering and leaving the building, and why. She was known around the colonia as the Goddess of Gab, as Tavo informed his parents. Gloria preferred to be discreet with Josefina, but the fact was that the woman knew far more about the residents of La Mascota than they liked to admit. If anyone was in the know about the comings and goings of the Miranda Felipe household since little Gloria's kidnapping, it was her. One neighbor moved out the day after it happened. Nearly all the others stopped by during the weeks that followed to offer assistance: a woman downstairs from them had offered to take care of the boys, but Consuelo was already doing that; she played with them as if she were a child herself, though it was just a shadow of what she might have done with her daughter Alicia in Tlalpujahua. Tavo had adopted the role of older brother to Consuelo, and sometimes circumstances made him take on the role of older brother to his own mother. Gloria was somewhere else. Her sons could sense it, they felt it. There was a different look in her eyes; her way of being around them had changed. She had the same blank stare that morning after her insomnia, but the doorbell rang again, bringing her back into the present, and she noticed the full glass of water resting on the radio—when had she left it there?—just as Josefina was saying through the door that two nuns were there to see her. In came the three women, Josefina and the nuns, the building administrator looking intently at Gloria and Tavo.

The taller nun, a strikingly tall woman with bony hands and fingers like dry reeds, said in a voice even deeper than Gustavo's: "Word of your troubles reached the convent, and we came to invite you to our chapel. Whenever you wish, we can pray together for your daughter. Our Order prays every morning to God our Father and the Virgin of Guadalupe for little Gloria, and we will continue to do so until she is found, Mrs. Felipe."

But what if someone called, what if someone had information for her and she was in the chapel praying with the nuns, or if she had to travel somewhere or do anything else related to the search for her daughter? The other nun, who was short with a bulbous nose and fingers that looked like meringue logs, quoted a passage from the Bible to comfort her. When Gloria received her first Holy Communion, she was called on in catechism to read unrelated passages from the Old and New Testaments, although it would be an exaggeration to call it reading because what she did was repeat the words like a parrot, a religious parrot, or at least a parrot that said "Amen" when everyone else did, and suddenly she recalled the story of Job and it was like looking in a mirror. Although, while we're on the subject, couldn't a parrot repeat the book of Job? Gloria knew she was avoiding the situation with this kind of question and asked herself others. She thought of Job because of his great misfortune and wondered how God

47

could be capable of such punishment. Why was God punishing her this way? Or was God actually Satan? Just like love, when taken to its extreme, is also hate, couldn't the greatest good also be evil? Why would Almighty God have allowed her daughter, who was barely two years old, to be ripped from her home, from her mother's arms, from her, to be taken so far from her breast, and now two nuns were there talking about the Bible? And what if her fate was the same as Job's? If God was going to test her faith with one tragedy after another like he did to Job? Could there be a worse scenario? Wasn't her situation already a worst-case scenario? Does evil exist inside good? Is God also Satan? This question shot through her like lightning and brought her back to the present with the nuns, perhaps to remind her that her thoughts and pain were not recognized by her surroundings, just like the night doesn't recognize lightning or thunder. The nun with fingers like meringue logs gestured with her hands as she said something about prayers, and her movements seemed to refer instead to a delicious recipe. Gloria thanked the nuns for their prayers and thanked all three women for their good intentions and was just about to have them out of her home when Josefina offered the nuns a glass of water and they accepted. Consuelo was making the beds, so Tavo brought the nun with chubby hands and the nun with fingers like dry reeds glasses of water, and Gloria stepped into the bathroom. She immediately noticed how haggard she looked and how bad she felt, but it didn't matter how much she hated the image in the mirror because what she was experiencing was worse: the discomfort of being herself, of being that thing in the mirror. Who was that?

Her mother told her that she couldn't just let herself go, that she needed to eat well, get enough rest, and see to her personal hygiene. Ana María had noticed her daughter losing weight and wanted to help, but she didn't know how. She had always expressed her maternal love by being a good provider. She adopted that role the day she left behind her life with the Spaniard whose name we will not speak. First with her daughter and her own mother, then with all the people who worked for her, and finally with anyone who crossed her path; she was known for tipping generously in the restaurants she frequented. Her daughter's present situation made her confront, for the first time in her life, how hard it was for her to offer physical affection. A hug, for example. A phone call without checking the clock, for example. Or spending time with her daughter without any particular plan. Instead, she gave her daughter a couple of tailored day dresses so she could look a bit nicer, even so thin. It also seemed like a good idea to give her cosmetics and a bottle of French perfume. A tube of red lipstick might restore some of her daughter's confidence. It goes without saying that Gloria stuck the unopened packages in a drawer in the bathroom. And she wore the dresses just like she used her body: dresses and body were simply things that were there and, well, she might as well use them. Inside and outside her home, her body and things needed to interact with other bodies and things. There was nothing to be done about it.

On March 20, 1946, an anonymous message arrived at the Miranda Felipe residence, along with the shoes little Gloria was wearing the day she was taken. The message described a corner in the historic district where a woman sold tamales and atole from five to ten in the morning. It was a busy corner, and a line usually formed before the sun was out. According to the message, the woman would leave two of her large pots on the ground; one would contain information about Gloria Miranda Felipe's whereabouts, and the other would be empty. Gloria Felipe spent the entire night clutching her daughter's shoe. There was a stain on it.

She couldn't tell if it was grease, blood, or something else, so she licked the stain. It didn't taste of iron, so she was almost certain that it wasn't blood. She prayed with that shoe in her hand as if it were a rosary that gave her hope, a sign that her daughter was alive. But the shoe didn't smell like it had been worn recently, and this detail stopped her heart. How long ago had her daughter's shoes been removed? How had they gotten stained? All these questions pained the same place in her. At the appointed hour, she would go to the corner hand in hand with her youngest son—the message was specific on this point—and deposit 25,000 pesos in small, unmarked bills in the empty tamale pot. She would wait twenty-four hours before getting her daughter at the address she would find in the other pot; this would give them time to leave the city. If she didn't wait, the typewritten message said, "We're not responsable for your kid's safety." She was to be there at six thirty the next morning.

Following the instructions of Captain Rubén Darío Hernández, as they had done before, she would hand over some real money mixed in with newspaper cut to look like the rest of the sum.

Rubén Darío and José Córdova, one of the few people who called the captain by his last name, watched the scene from the corner facing the tamale vendor as they smoked their first cigarettes of the morning. Hernández had a craving for one of those tamales and some atole; the line was really long, which meant they must be good. They talked about busy spots and long lines, both guarantees of good food, but they were on duty, said Hernández, and couldn't be buying tamales at a time like this. He wanted to make a good impression on Córdova, who never seemed to think about food, and changed the topic while they kept their eyes on Gloria Felipe, who looked nervous standing there, holding hands with little Carlos as instructed.

In line, Carlos was trying to talk with his mother, but she ignored him. Her thoughts were very far from the child whose hand she was holding. The little boy eventually got her attention by blurting out: "And if I get kidnapped, will you pay attention to me, Mommy? Do you want them to take me, too? I want to be kidnapped so you'll pay attention to me."

Gloria was supposed to say a simple code word to the vendor so that in addition to the two tamales she ordered—one green, one sweet—she would pass her the pots on the ground next to her so that Gloria could take one of them off to the side and fill it with small bills, just like the anonymous message indicated. After the vendor gave Gloria her tamales, she asked if she needed help carrying the pot. That was when Captain Rubén Darío Hernández detained her. On his orders, she gave the pot with the girl's location to the reporter—who thought it weighed an awful lot for a pot filled with just information, maybe there were some stones holding the paper down—as she confessed to the captain that a man had given her the two pots to pass on to a woman with a five-year-old boy who would order two special breakfasts at six thirty in the morning, and had paid her 200 pesos for her trouble. Many people in line had dispersed, chattering about what had happened, but most had remained, waiting for the police to let the tamale vendor get back to selling her wares.

As Captain Rubén Darío Hernández and José Córdova were leaving Gloria Felipe and her son Carlos in the doorway of their building, the reporter mentioned that the pot seemed strangely heavy.

"Let's open it over there," said Hernández, "in that vacant lot."

When they opened the pot, they found explosives inside—the kind fishermen used years ago, before the rivers of Mexico City all dried into pollution-stained streets and avenues. Luckily, they had enough time to get some distance between themselves and the explosion.

As they watched the pot smolder, the scale of the case suddenly hit the reporter, who turned to Hernández and said, "These guys have done some pretty bad shit, come up with some ingenious ways of making off with the ransom money, but this is a whole other thing. Trying to hurt the parents of a kidnapped girl, that just says all bets are off."

Evil may seem limitless, but it is never infinite.

6.

IN THE LAST WEEK OF MARCH 1946 ALONE, THREE children had been kidnapped like Gloria Miranda Felipe from different states in Northern Mexico: a newborn, a three-year-old girl, and a five-year-old boy. The news distressed Nuria Valencia, who had a nervous temperament before Agustina came into her life; now, her anxiety was through the roof. On a brighter note, Agustina had started calling Nuria's parents "grandma" and "grandpa" instead of their given names.

Martín Fernández worked in the office of one of the movie theaters downtown. He didn't care much for moving pictures. Before that, he had worked as a floor manager at a supermarket, where he would have liked to have been promoted, but he saw an ad for the job at the cinema and it seemed like a good opportunity. The difference in his salary wouldn't be huge, but the extra money would come in handy, especially now that he and Nuria had a family to support. His mother, Agustina Mendía, lived in Xochimilco, which was all the way at the outskirts of the city back then, but they had a close relationship despite the distance and saw each other often. Martín thought his mother was the greatest talent to ever grace a kitchen and often made comments comparing Nuria's cooking unfavorably to hers. We should have my mother come over and give you lessons, he said once after Nuria burned a flan.

Nuria Valencia worked full-time as the secretary of a doctor at the public hospital. More specifically, she was the secretary of General Hospital's most famous cardiologist. It's best not to go around using that word so much, but in this case it's simply stating a fact: her employer was a famous doctor, respected by his peers and admired by politicians and high society alike. He was regularly invited to speak at conferences in Mexico and abroad. He sat on the Board of Public Health, an authority connected to the presidency, and was in a position to make health policy decisions for the entire country during a grand period of development. He was often invited to galas and dinners at the highest level of national politics, held a seat on the faculty of cardiology at the national public university, was called in to consult on cases at the Children's Hospital of Mexico, and had two assistants at General Hospital: one who kept his social and political calendar—that was Nuria's colleague, Constanza—and one who saw to his responsibilities at the hospital. That was the position Nuria had held for years: her first and only job.

The cardiologist's office was a perfect reflection of his personality: in the large foyer there was a scale, metal cabinets painted with beige enamel that contained his tools and medical materials, a black leather examination bed, and several classic anatomical illustrations of the human body and heart. From that bed, or from the reclinable chair where he also conducted examinations, his patients got a clear view of the numerous diplomas, awards, and recognitions that he displayed in a semicircle like a peacock's plumage. In the back right corner was a hallway that led to his study and was like a condensed version of his home: family photos of him with his wife and daughters, the weddings of his two daughters—the in-laws were missing from both pictures; it was only him with the brides. There was also an oil portrait of him and his wife with their daughters when the girls were still young and a few plants on his desk, supported by little plates and coasters placed there by his wife so they wouldn't damage the wood. It was like stepping into his living room. And that was how the cardiologist seemed to be divided between his public and private life, as if they were two spaces divided by some kind of border that he passed back and forth through all the time as if they were, ultimately, the same. He was respectful with his assistant and his secretary and knew what was going on in their lives; his excellent memory was an important part of his character—he would pick up conversations with people he hadn't seen in a long time exactly where they had left off, as if he were playing multiple games of chess at the same time and knew at any given moment where all the pieces were and why they were there. He had excellent recall and cared about people's family lives—he himself was a family man—and that, in addition to inspiring respect, made him well-liked. He did this with the hospital staff he would see around his office, in the hallways, or in the operating room. He asked about their children, their partners or spouses, and the last topic they had discussed. Using the power he had, he had helped many people over the years. Decades later, at the funeral of this beloved cardiologist, the room would be overflowing with politicians, public servants, colleagues and friends from the hospital, and, above all, the countless blue-collar workers he helped in a thousand small ways, like the hospital employee who couldn't squeeze inside to attend the service but who was grateful for the money the doctor had given her to pay her son's matriculation fees at school.

The cardiologist knew about Nuria's desire to be a mother; he referred her to the most respected specialists in obstetrics and gynecology, and the fact that she worked for him opened doors for her at the orphanage. The bureaucracy there was labyrinthine and seemed designed to prevent couples from adopting a child. Given her age—thirty-four at the time—she was considered "too old," as she had been told before, to adopt a newborn. Younger couples had priority, but she was eligible to participate in a program run by the orphanage because she worked in health services and because she was in a position to offer a better quality of life to an orphan for a few days, having been preselected by the institution's administrative board. In other words—and with my apologies for going off on a tangent—children were allowed to spend time with certain families outside the orphanage.

One autumn afternoon, just over a year before she finally brought Agustina home, Nuria Valencia was allowed to spend a weekend with an eight-year-old boy named Efraín. If everything went according to their agreement with the orphanage, Nuria and Martín could spend more weekends with him.

Efraín knew nothing about the people we'll call his biological parents. All he retained from his infancy was a little silver chain with a small round amulet of the Virgin of Guadalupe that might have been put on him by his mother, his father, his grandparents, a nun, or a nurse, he had no idea. No one could tell him, and he'd grown up with that little chain around his neck as if it were an extension of his body, clinging to the only remaining thing from his past, hoping that someone, someday, would know who gave it to him and solve the mystery of his origin. His earliest memories were from the orphanage; all his dreams and nightmares had occurred on the metal-framed single bed in the large room he shared with many other children under the age of thirteen; in most of his dreams, the orphanage was his home, though there were a few in which the orphanage was a real home, a house and not an institution, and there were even some where it was a store and he was for sale but no one wanted to buy him, and he just sat there like a pile of overripe guavas slowly turning to pulp. The reason this happened, in reality rather than in his dream, as the nuns had told him on the two occasions they'd discussed the topic, was that people tended not to adopt children who arrived after infancy, and he had been three years old already, though he had no memory of anything before the orphanage. Most couples wanted newborns—those went quickly, in a matter of weeks, or months if the paperwork got held up.

Efraín had a wall eye, difficulty controlling his bladder, and two tics about which a nun informed Nuria Valencia before she met him: when he got scared, his knees would begin to shake and he would bite his lower lip, sometimes until it bled. Martín didn't like the idea of having Efraín spend the weekend with them, he didn't like the situation in general, but what could he do? It was the closest they could get to being parents at the moment, and Nuria had assured him that this would bring them a step closer to adopting. It will give us points with the board, she told her husband as she bit into a green pear as crisp as a new chapter.

The night Efraín arrived at Nuria and Martín's house, he stuffed himself with pastries and hot chocolate. At 2:40 a.m. he got up to vomit. He didn't manage to get the door to the bathroom open in time, and when Nuria explained this to Martín he just groaned and rolled over. Nuria brought the boy into the kitchen, explained why he'd gotten sick, and gave him some chamomile tea with anise and a spoonful of sodium bicarbonate in a glass of water, which he was able to keep down. In bed, she told him a story as she stroked his hair, and before the boy fell asleep she said that if he felt sick again, he should wake her. He was staying in the room Nuria reserved for her parents when they came to visit, or for Martín's mother if she didn't want to return too late to Xochimilco.

Nuria had a hard time falling asleep that night, and in her insomnia she thought about how much she had wanted to be a mother, how much she had idealized it, and how on the very first night she spent with a child in her home, he had vomited on the wood floors and stained the door to their only bathroom. But wasn't that just life? Wasn't that what being a mother was about? Waking up in the middle of the night to clean up vomit before the smell soaked into the parquet, soothing the child and giving him something to settle his stomach, sitting with him until he fell back asleep? After all, thought Nuria, it's lovely to take care of someone, and even though her husband had found the scene unfortunate, for her it was the sweet honey of what she had longed for all those years, what had seemed so impossible. She was lost in these thoughts when Martín woke up and asked if she'd cleaned up "that boy's mess." Why did he have to draw that line between them and the child? Why was he angry? But instead of posing these questions to him, Nuria was sweet and placating with her husband.

Efraín, thought Nuria, was a sad and lovely boy, and she would have loved to keep him, not just for that day or that weekend, but for his whole life, to take away his sadness and show him all the beauty she saw in him. Love, thought Nuria, fixes everything. And among these soft, diaphanous thoughts that changed shape like clouds, she fell asleep. In the morning, the boy called them Mister and Missus, and Nuria wished he would call them Papá and Mamá, but there was no way to ask for that. Instead, she asked him to call them by their names, which he tried to do, but his knees started trembling. When the child was in the bathroom, Martín asked Nuria quietly what was wrong with his eyes and whether it could be cured. While she summarized the report she'd been given about Efraín, a seed began to sprout somewhere inside Nuria and it grew in fast motion until a simple five-petaled flower emerged. She decided to ask her employer to help her get the boy's strabismus corrected at the Children's Hospital.

On the second night, Efraín wet the bed and Nuria soaked the sheets and blanket in soapy water, making it very clear that nothing was wrong and that what mattered was overcoming it eventually, because washing linens was nothing compared to how important it was that he feel safe there. The fact is that the boy felt very comfortable with Nuria, but not at all with Martín, and his body language made that abundantly clear. That night, Nuria got the idea to ask Efraín what he wanted to be when he grew up. No one had ever asked him that before; it seemed like his fate was to be an orphan forever, that even if he formed his own family, he would still be an orphan. His answer was spontaneous and sincere: "I want to be a professional soccer player so everyone will scream my name."

On Sunday afternoon, Martín proposed that they take a walk around the Zócalo and the historic district and later bought them all churros. Efraín took his hand as they crossed a broad street, and this little gesture softened Martín toward him. From that moment on, he was friendlier toward the boy, and by the time they sat down with their churros, he seemed to have changed his mind about him. It was the first time Efraín had eaten churros; he told Nuria that it was the happiest day of his life, and Martín didn't know what to do with that; it was as if someone had given him a box that was too big, too heavy, too everything for him to carry and he needed to leave it there on the floor, even though it contained a gift meant for him.

On the third night, Nuria decided to read Efraín to sleep

from a book of stories written by "international" authors, all of whom were white European men with narrators made in their image—these days, luckily, there's more variety among those who hold this job, if you're wondering. Both were excited and happy, one reading and the other listening. They drew the evening out, reading like that until after eleven; then Efraín started asking obvious questions, like someone bouncing a ball just for the sake of it until he fell asleep after midnight. Nuria was tired, too, but more than that, she felt happy at the sight of the boy lying in the guest bedroom, which she had spent years imagining as the bedroom of her own child. Finally, a small, warm body smelling of clean sheets and the pajamas she had bought for the boy the day she went to pick him up at the orphanage. As she got into bed beside her sleeping husband, a huge wave of sorrow knocked her suddenly into silent tears that went as unnoticed as a nocturnal breeze. It had made her so sad when Efraín, with his strabismus, told her that he wanted to be a professional soccer player. Maybe he was hoping that his parents would recognize him at the height of his fame. Or that, even if his parents hadn't loved him, maybe the rest of the world could. That night, Nuria calmed herself by reciting an Ave Maria, the prayer her own mother had often used to soothe her.

Monday morning was sad for both of them. Efraín had felt cared for and loved by Nuria. Had the choice been his, he would have stayed there forever; this would have pleased Nuria and made Martín uncomfortable at first, but he would eventually have come to accept him, even to love him, and it would have taken Efraín a long time to build up his confidence. In any case, this was not the path any of them would take and they seemed to sense it, even though they all wished for it in their own way. So it was a melancholy farewell, especially for Efraín and Nuria, who had each opened a wound that connected them by a bond more intimate than that of mother and child—maybe because sharing a profound pain with someone creates a connection beyond hierarchical relations. From the orphanage, Nuria went to work at the hospital, thinking all the way about asking her employer to help get Efraín's strabismus corrected in the Children's Hospital.

Constanza was ten years younger than Nuria and was the single mother of a two-and-a-half-year-old child that she left at a daycare center near work. She had slept three times with a medical student doing his residency at the hospital; the afternoon she got pregnant, they had gone into a storage closet and she hadn't taken off her clothes. He dropped his pants, and Constanza heard some change fall out. Later, she would have a clearer memory of that sound than of what she had felt. She raised her skirt, he lowered his underwear; they didn't kiss on the mouth during the three or four minutes they had sex, and then she never heard from him again. It was an absolute scandal, a dishonor to the entire family, but they ended up accepting the child in their home and her mother told her that her cross to bear for having a child out of wedlock would be to work like a dog for the rest of her life. That would be her punishment. Constanza often spoke about her son as a burden, and it sometimes made Nuria uncomfortable that the thing she most desired would be viewed as a punishment by someone she saw every day.

Nuria had gotten used to the sensation of being the one left standing in a game of musical chairs: while everyone else danced around in a circle, waiting to rush for a seat the moment the music stopped, she watched from a corner, knowing she had no place in the game. Constanza would say things to her like, "You're so lucky not to have kids, you get to rest on the weekends," or she would complain about how her parents didn't want to look after him sometimes when she wanted to go to a party or a little gathering, or else she just complained in general about having a child, tossing out some observation or another about how much better it was not to. Nuria, on the other hand, was reserved with her coworker and barely discussed her personal life with her. For a long time, Constanza thought Nuria was single. She pictured her living with and caring for her elderly mother, who was also alone, widowed, and was surprised when Nuria's husband called one day while she was in the bathroom. Constanza gave her the message, adding that she hadn't known Nuria was married. "You certainly hold your cards close to your chest," she said, with her fingers and eyes glued to her typewriter, hiding her envy at the fact that Nuria had what she wanted: a man to call her husband. The word seemed to her like snow itself, so impossible in her present reality in Mexico City, belonging to some distant, happy Christmas landscape, one she might never get to experience, much less with a fatherless son in tow.

The doctor hadn't been able to attend Nuria and Martín's wedding, but he had given them one of their most exquisite wedding gifts: a hand-painted set of plates. Nuria didn't tend to talk about her personal life; the doctor had picked up on little signs and got to know her wishes without her needing to express them directly. One day he saw her interact with a little boy in the hallway, and another time he saw her reading about mothers and children. Yet another time, he noticed that she flinched slightly when Constanza said something about her son. A series of moments that added up, like Morse code, into a message. He told Nuria that if she wanted to have children, perhaps he could refer her to a specialist he knew; that comment was like a door Nuria would never have thought to open herself, but when she saw it standing open in front of her, she realized just how big it was. Nuria worked up the courage to voice her desire. She trusted the cardiologist, and after the weekend they had Efraín with them, she found a moment to mention that the boy suffered from strabismus and that maybe he would have a better chance of being adopted if it could be fixed, since it was already so hard for children his age to find homes. Her employer didn't hesitate. He told her that yes, of course, the boy probably needed only a simple surgery, and he offered his medical and bureaucratic support throughout the process, which was his way of supporting Nuria, since family was his axis mundi.

That afternoon, Nuria went back to the orphanage and told all this to the same nun who had told her about Efraín's conditions. May God bless you, said the nun, and asked if Nuria wanted to tell Efraín the news. His convalescence after the operation was spent at Nuria and Martín's house. Martín was surprised how quickly everything had happened and was glad to have the child at home. One day he came back from work at the movie theater with a kaleidoscope. So you can try out your eyes, he said. He also brought a bag of the churros Efraín had liked so much.

The first two nights her daughter Agustina spent at home, Nuria felt an immense love that seemed to expand inside her, and in the process, to expand her. She couldn't put it into words and had no desire to do so. She felt drunk on love. And that feeling was enough. Even though she had been with Martín many years, the love she felt in this situation seemed somehow greater, as if it were being rounded out, completed. Coming full circle, like the sun. Those first nights, she stroked Agustina's arms and forehead until the little girl fell asleep, and that simple act filled her like a cup that with just a little water, barely any, would overflow. The third night Agustina spent with them, in the guest room they had hastily set up as hers, Nuria took in the scent of her hair for hours after she fell asleep. It smelled a bit like milk, a bit like soap, and a bit like orange blossom; all of it together—the lamp giving off its warm light on the nightstand as if it were giving off the same soft smell as her daughter, Augustina's small form in the bed, much smaller even than Efraín's—reconciled her with the sadness she had felt when Efraín slept in that bed for the last time after his eye operation, knowing that she had done all she could for the child and that their time together was coming to an end. Now, seeing Agustina there, in that same bed, which was now hers, Nuria thanked God for giving her that chance. She felt happy. How was it possible to feel so much happiness, so much love, she wondered, as if she were drunk on the perfectly mundane life she had, on just watching her daughter sleep. Nuria had made peace with her past, but their current context, all those kidnappings, stirred an anxiety in her that grew every day alongside her love. Maybe because love contains a large measure of fear. Fear and love are not separate things; on the contrary, they're like two fires. One doubles the other. And if love contains a large measure of fear, what should we do with that redoubled fire?

7.

THREE MONTHS AFTER GLORIA MIRANDA FELIPE'S
kidnapping, Josefina, the building administrator, knocked on the
Miranda Felipe family's door with a note in her hand. Gustavo
Miranda opened the door. Josefina said something to him about a
rumor she'd heard who knows where that seemed to have something to do with his daughter.

Gustavo began to read the note as he closed the door: "To the
parents of Gloria Miranda: we have your daughter. Don't worry,
she is well fed and well taken care of. If you don't tell the police this time what you're doing, you can have her back. One of
you two should go to the Cathedral with three sunflowers in your
hand; if I or anyone with me sees a police officer, your daughter
is as good as dead. If you give me a cardboard box with thirty
thousand pesos, you will receive at your home another typewritten note with the address and time where you can retrieve your
daughter. If you follow these instructions exactly, you will have
her with you again." Before leaving for work, while his wife was
still sleeping and his sons were eating Consuelo's sweetened oat-
meal with banana Tavo had cut up for them, Gustavo spoke with
Ana María, who was already in her atelier. Then he called Captain
Rubén Darío Hernández on his direct line.

Hernández cradled the receiver between his shoulder and his ear as he ate a tamal with one hand and stirred sugar into his coffee with the other; at that early hour, as Gustavo spoke, the captain's shirt collected its first stains of the day. His instructions remained the same: the money was to be mixed with fake currency, and they needed clues that could lead them to the kidnappers. Ana María also spoke with Hernández. She was willing to spend as much money as necessary to get her granddaughter back. It took her all of a minute and a half to gather the sum plus a bribe for Hernández, who made a joke that left Ana María confused about whether or not he had accepted it.

Years earlier, Ana María Felipe lost the twins she was carrying. The Spaniard—whose name we will not speak—had locked her in a rooftop storage room after beating and kicking her; he had stormed off, insulting her, cursing her and the day she'd fallen pregnant a second time. Ana María watched herself bleeding to death. The world shrank to the size of that room. She felt herself losing the pregnancy. She felt it and she saw it and she knew; her screams turned to howls louder than the street noise and a neighbor came to see what was happening. She thought someone was slaughtering an animal, but when she realized it was Ana María wailing in pain, she wrapped a towel around her fist and broke the glass to free her. She brought her to the clinic, where they were able to stabilize her. Ana María lost her twins in that rooftop storage room, learning only in that moment that there had been two babies inside her, while her five-year-old daughter Gloria was locked in a room downstairs by the Spaniard whose name we will not speak. The neighbor had gotten her and left her with her husband and children while she was in the clinic with Ana María. The next day, the man who was still Ana María's husband was drunk somewhere and still drinking, while her neighbor watched

over her recovery in the clinic. Ana María would feel more gratitude toward this neighbor than anyone else, but it was hard for her
to spend time with her after what had happened, and she stopped
seeing her because she reminded her of the worst day of her life.
Anyway, during the few hours of sleep she had gotten in the clinic
with the help of intravenous painkillers, she had dreamed of losing her twins in that rooftop storage room. Dream and reality
formed an unbearable mirror.

How could she let her daughter lose her granddaughter, after
she lost the twins? Impossible. She would do anything. Her resources weren't infinite, but they were limitless when it came to
finding her only granddaughter, the only one in the family who
inherited the freckles that dotted her arms, shoulders, and back
like a constellation unique to the two of them, perhaps like twins
born decades apart. Or maybe Ana María felt like she was rescu-
ing herself as a girl, saving little Gloria from the harsh destiny of
going barefoot like she had. Her granddaughter looked just like
her at that age; if they had occupied the same time and space, it
would have been impossible to tell them apart. She realized this
the first day she held her. What a strange twist of fate, to have lost
twins at the age of twenty-eight, only to be handed a granddaughter identical to her, a twin of her own, when she was nearly sixty.
There was no way Ana María was going to allow a baby, another
baby, the daughter of her daughter, her only granddaughter, to be
taken from her the way her twins were taken on that rooftop.

Ana María Felipe told Beatriz to attend to her clients that
morning and went to speak in person with Captain Rubén Darío
Hernández of Special Operations. She was explicit about the bribe
because she didn't want to lose any more time, but she asked him
not to tell her daughter and son-in-law. She was tired of handing
over small sums to extortionists who brought them no closer to

67

Gloria. She needed to be proactive and pull any strings necessary until they found her.

"Put someone on my granddaughter's case full-time," she ordered with lips painted crimson red. "Or are you profiting somehow from stringing us along? I certainly hope not."

Captain Rubén Darío Hernández replied that he had other cases to solve, cases just as important as little Gloria's, but that he was investigating the matter himself.

"How much do you need to make my granddaughter's case a priority, to find her once and for all?" insisted Ana María, eyeing the stains on the captain's shirt. "You are aware that this case has the media in a frenzy," she continued, "so it would be in your best interest to solve it as soon as possible. You don't need to answer right away, you know how to reach me, but think about it. Name your price. For now, here's three thousand pesos to go out and buy the most expensive sunflowers in the city, but listen carefully, Rubén Darío Hernández, look me in the eyes and listen carefully. You *will* get me my granddaughter back." And Ana María Felipe walked out, leaving behind a thick trail of French perfume.

Two Poems asked his supervisor for authorization to put Rodríguez Guardiola on Gloria Miranda Felipe's case full-time, a request that was denied before Rubén Darío could even get it out of his mouth. Then he met up with José Córdova and asked for his help with the investigation. *Collaboration* was the word he used as he ate his noontime second breakfast of lip-smacking chilaquiles in green sauce—man, I could really go for a plate of those right now—while Córdova drank a cup of black coffee without sugar. The reporter accepted half of the money Ana María had just given to Hernández.

That time it was Gustavo Miranda who went with three sunflowers in his hand to the cathedral in the Zócalo, where someone would supposedly be waiting for him, though he wasn't sure if it would be a man or a woman, or how he would know who it was. After around fifteen minutes, a man appeared who might have been twice Gustavo's age: haggard and thin in white pants, a white shirt, and a hat, with the melancholy gaze of a bolero singer. He was headed straight for Gustavo. It was him. The man asked for the sunflowers, and Gustavo took him literally. He also handed over the cardboard box with the currency and paper mixed together so it looked like the full ransom. José Córdova, who was not known to be collaborating with the police, whistled, and Two Poems detained the man, who tried to defend himself with the sunflowers, creating a comical scene in which the yellow petals went flying like tears of laughter. But it was also sad, especially for Gustavo Miranda, because this was clearly just another fraud. At police headquarters, they soon learned that they'd apprehended an old extortionist who had just been released from Lecumberri Prison after serving time for robbery, extortion, and bank fraud. His record indicated that he also been caught carrying weapons, including four pocketknives in the soles of his shoes and the brim of his hat, discovered after one of his robberies. Two Poems made a few jokes about his use of sunflowers to defend himself, but Córdova did not find them amusing. The criminal confessed after just a few hours in the precinct, wearing a sad face—an expression he seemed to have been born with, as if he lamented his existence and, while he was at it, the existence of the whole world and everything in it—that he needed money, and the girl's case seemed like an easy way to get some. Captain Rubén Darío Hernández handcuffed him and ordered Octavio, his colleague with a cleft lip and rigorously polished boots, to take him straight back to the Black Palace. On his way in, the captain had dropped the extra sunflowers, the ones left over from the dozen he'd bought for the operation, on the desk of a colleague near the door, and now he shouted at the man that he wanted them back.

"Here you go, poet," said the officer, and handed them over, muttering something else under his breath, uncomfortable to be giving another man flowers.

Rubén Darío's father had given him that name because he admired the Nicaraguan enough after reading just a few of his poems to name his firstborn after him and to name his daughter Azul Hernández. He had been a police officer, too, though he never ranked as high as his son, and at the time he'd believed that naming his boy after the King of Latin American Poetry and his daughter after The Poem would broaden their horizons. And it was certainly true that Rubén Darío Hernández paid special attention in his literature class as a teenager; he still had the copy of the complete works of Rubén Darío that he'd bought back then for a few cents in a used bookstore. He also kept several volumes of poetry in his office and occasionally leafed through them, particularly when he wanted to clear his mind. The fact that a police officer would have secondhand books of poetry, including one that had been with him since adolescence—which is to say, a book he clearly cared about; at the precinct he was like a shoe without its mate, a police officer caring about a fucking poetry book, what the hell was that—was a source of rumors among his peers, a snowball-turned-avalanche that followed him around wherever he went, and the reason he was called Two Poems. Sometimes they also called him the Poet, Two Tacos, or Two Problems, among other things. He had even memorized Ramón López Velarde's "La suave patria" at one point and liked to recite it. He was a little rusty lately, but he could still get a few verses out if he tried. At his wedding, he had recited a Spanish translation of one of Shakespeare's love sonnets, compiled in a volume titled *Beautiful Love*

Poems, bringing tears to the eyes of his wife and mother-in-law. Sometimes he drew in the margins of his notebook while he was on the phone. He liked singing in the shower and whistling the latest tunes. He was a good dancer, better than his wife, and could liven up the dance floor all by himself, clapping, moving his hips, and sometimes even doing little jumps to get people going; that was his secret weapon when it was time to get the crowd moving. His father was convinced he'd inherited his artistic streak from his name and not his bloodline. Had he been a wrestler, he probably would have gone with Rubén Darío "The Poet" Hernández, that was how much he liked his name, and he would have created a comically exaggerated character to match, maybe one who entered the ring with a flower clamped between his teeth because, far from being offended, the captain was delighted when someone pointed out his artistic inclinations. If anyone left sunflowers, a book, or a piece of paper covered with doodles on a desk at headquarters, everyone knew it belonged to Captain Rubén Darío Hernández.

Four months had passed since Gloria Miranda Felipe had been kidnapped, and Hernández still had no sense of her whereabouts or those of the other kidnapped children. Not a moment went by that Gloria Felipe didn't feel empty inside; she often prayed with her daughter's little shoe in her hands. She had been suffering from insomnia for months and had a panic attack in the kitchen one day while her youngest was doing an assignment. Carlos started to cry and shouted to his older brothers that their mother was dying. More than 2,500 images of Gloria Miranda Felipe, now two years and four months old, circulated along the country's northern and southern borders and around police stations, but the officers of Special Operations had no more clues than they did on the day she was taken, which is to say, none.

But then the main line at Special Operations rang, and

someone asked for Hernández. On the other end of the connection was a familiar voice, an old police officer from Oaxaca.

"Cabrón," he said, "the girl's in Juchitán. They're about to take her across the border to sell her off on the other side. Get your ass down here."

Rubén Darío called his wife and asked him to go with him, then he asked two police officers—Rodríguez Guardiola and Octavio—to do the same. He alerted his boss, Ana María, but he did not call the Miranda Felipe household. They were on the highway by four that afternoon.

As they drove, thunder began to rumble and a heavy curtain of rain obscured the road ahead of them. What frightened Hernández's wife most was how the trees shook in the storm, and she said so as she looked out the passenger window. Octavio was terrified; as he watched the branches whip violently in the wind, he thought it was the angriest he had ever seen nature and felt like a child again. Hernández tried to turn at a crossroads and the car flipped over. It took them a long time to get the doors open. The storm wasn't letting up, and the trees shook with fury. Octavio was certain he was stuck in some horror story and was more afraid than Hernández's wife. They finally managed to get out of the car and set it back on the road. The four of them were soaked and it was nearly midnight before they reached the city of Oaxaca. They slept in a modest hotel and left in the morning for Juchitán with the police officer who had called them there. They found the house where a short woman with a gruff, imposing demeanor was watching a fairly large group of children. She insisted that she was keeping an eye on them as a favor to several mothers in the neighborhood. There were seven boys and eight girls. The woman didn't want to let them in, but she eventually had to give in to the curiosity of the children, who wanted to know who was at the door. Hernández handed the woman a photograph. She agreed that one of her girls did look a lot like little Gloria, but without the freckles, and with darker skin. The child's name was Natalia. Hernández's wife was most struck by the resemblance. She spoke with Natalia for a while, as if she were a stand-in for the girl they were trying to find. They were even the same age. That night, Captain Rubén Darío Hernández returned to Mexico City with his wife and the two other police officers.

Hernández called Ana María to recount the details of their trip to Oaxaca. His enthusiasm when describing Natalia's resemblance to her granddaughter disturbed her, and she felt the need to change the subject and inform him that they had prepared a new message, which announced an even higher reward for anyone who could lead them to little Gloria. Money was no object, she said, then reminded Rubén Darío of the bribe she had paid to speed things up.

It was no secret how Ana María Felipe had made her fortune. She had given several interviews on the subject, in magazines and the society pages. Newspaper articles had been written about her—her travels and lifestyle, which was truly unusual for a woman of her time. Back then, Gloria had struggled with Ana María's public persona. Socialites, politicians' wives, theater and film actresses, and wealthy women in general sought out Ana María's designs, which were inspired by her clients; she made their dresses according to the personality and taste of each, based on their conversations. You might say that she was, first and foremost, a designer who listened to her clients and genuinely enjoyed developing relationships with them beyond their professional interactions. She had a unique approach to her work, and her reputation grew; word spread in Mexico and abroad, which brought her even more clients. But a daughter is a daughter, and the idea

73

of a mother is the idea of a mother, and Gloria Felipe had felt on several occasions that her mother was not there for her.

Ana María Felipe was born at the end of the nineteenth century. Her father was old, and her mother was young. Like a story from the Bible, the man—who was already in his sixties—learned he would be a father when his right ear was beginning to fail him. He had his first and only daughter and he also had enough money to pay for her to be tutored in embroidery, sewing, piano, and gardening, because the most important thing, he thought, was to raise an ideal future housewife who could name flowers, play the piano, and cook delicious meals. Ana María didn't learn how to read until she needed the skill in her first job and taught herself. In those days, women did not have access to higher education or the right to vote, which is to say that Ana María grew up in a world where a woman's highest aspiration was to become a housewife, full stop. And her father wanted to give her the tools she needed to be the best.

Ana María's father died of kidney failure when she was thirteen years old. His hearing loss late in life inspired her to play the piano more and more, because it gave him pleasure. After he died, she ended up playing accompaniment for silent movies in order to make money; she was paid less than her male counterparts, but it was one of the few things she knew how to do that would allow her to earn enough to support herself and her mother. Upon her father's unexpected death, one of his sisters had found a way to have Ana María and her mother removed from his will, so Ana María supported her mother from the age of thirteen.

She first started playing piano in a silent movie theater one rainy summer afternoon—the summer rains are one thing climate change hasn't affected, thankfully, since they're something I, as the third-person narrator of this story, especially like about

74

Mexico City; I mention this because at this very moment it's raining just like it rained the afternoon Ana María sat down at a piano in the cinema for the first time to accompany a silent film. She got along well with the young man she alternated shifts with, who was a few years older than her. One day, they got to talking about what they liked to do, and Ana María told him that she dreamed of making the clothes she drew in her notebook. He suggested that she talk with his wife, who worked in a clothing store where they also made nightgowns and women's attire. The idea appealed to Ana María, who decided to give it a try. By the time she was sixteen, she was already garnering attention for her remarkable handiwork; she learned how to work with lace and perfected her sewing skills with the wife of her former colleague. After just over a year, she had such an impressive reputation that they promoted her to day wear, where she began working on dresses. It might go without saying, but decades after she accompanied silent films to support her and her mother, Ana María kept a piano in her home and although she rarely touched it, when she did play, it was like a game for her; something about the act reminded her of a safe place in her childhood and the sense of complicity she enjoyed with her father. Though music wasn't ultimately her path, she was grateful to have had such a gentle introduction to working. Ana María's mother also learned how to embroider, sequin, and bead, and she helped her daughter with the details of several pieces that made Ana María a favorite at the factory. So much so that the owner asked her the favor of making a few dresses for his wife. And this was how her entry to the Mount Olympus of the factory foreshadowed her future Olympus.

With the money she managed to save from making patterns for nightgowns and dresses, occasionally adding little touches of her own whenever she was allowed, Ana María proposed to her mother that they rent a small space where they could do the hair and nails of women in the neighborhood while she continued making clothes. The first space she was able to rent cost just a few pesos each month and could fit exactly two clients, which was how many Ana María's mother could see at a time. They put up a sign written in all capital letters that read ANA MARÍA BEAUTY PARLOR. And that was how, between the two of them, they were able to save enough money for Ana María to quit her job at the factory and work full-time at the salon. Her mother always knew her daughter was good with people. A gift, she would say whenever a client praised her pleasant demeanor, Ana María has a gift. More clients arrived when she began working full-time at the salon, and they found that they needed to rent a bigger space and hire a girl to help them with styling. While her mother focused on manicures and pedicures, Ana María was best with haircuts. She also chatted with her clients; she would be talking with one, and another would often jump into the conversation. Those were years Ana María remembered fondly; she had enjoyed her mother's company, and the truth of it was that they both had enjoyed working in the beauty parlor. As a secondary effect of that work, Ana María noticed that her mother felt useful for the first time in her life, and that had given her a certain lightness; it had made her radiant like the midday sun. Their temperaments had aligned, but Ana María really shone. And she would shine even more in the years to come, reaching incredible heights for her time.

Ana María drew her designs every night, just like she'd been doing since she was ten or eleven years old, but she had no money to make them. She imagined one woman, then another, wearing a particular evening gown. And she drew. One day, she left her notebook open on the counter at the beauty parlor, and one of

76

their clients asked Ana María to make the design to measure for her. So she did, suffering the whole time from what today we call impostor syndrome. This client, who would become a friend and a mentor to Ana María, was also the one who invited her to the party where she met the Spaniard whose name we will not speak. Ana María gave birth to her daughter Gloria at twenty-three, and at twenty-eight she lost twins after being beaten, and this client was the first person she called to ask for help. The client had a friend who needed a wedding gown, quickly, and she put the two women in touch.

Recently divorced, with a daughter who asked more questions than she could answer and a mother who helped with childcare during the day and sewing at night, Ana María made her first wedding gown. The bride appeared in a corner of the society pages, and between that publicity and the party itself, Ana María landed five new clients that year. Together with the money that came in from the salon, they were able to stay afloat.

Her story took an upward turn and just kept rising. She enjoyed making photo albums—one for each year, embossed with her initials in golden letters, which was the color of her self-esteem as she neared sixty—of her trips around the world to visit her suppliers of fabric, silks, lace, and buttons that looked like jewels at all the most-photographed parties. Her mother saved nearly every mention of her daughter's work from newspapers and magazines; she kept these clippings in a metal box that, over time, became several metal boxes organized by date. By the time her granddaughter was kidnapped, if one name was synonymous with fine gowns, it was Ana María's. Her shops were well-known. As was her unorthodox private life.

It was no secret that she wanted to buy the services of Captain Rubén Darío Hernández, just like corruption among the police force was no secret. The fact that she had raised the reward that day meant she had offered even more money to Hernández. It also created the possibility that anyone interested in conning her out of the reward money was going to invent more and more creative stories to get it. Word had spread among certain criminal elements that it was like shooting ducks in a barrel. Ana María's tendency to fix things with money like the good provider she was had made Gloria uncomfortable for as long as she could remember. Her surname was an umbilical cord that attached her to her mother, dragging along everything that weighed on her most. It pained her that she had an absent father and a famous mother who had made a fortune that allowed her to fix almost anything, and the desperation she felt over not being able to find her daughter sent her crashing back into what had hurt her so deeply a long time ago and had even sparked arguments with her mother on several occasions.

When she was a teenager, especially, Gloria had wondered why she couldn't have a traditional mother who didn't work, one who spent her time cooking and doing housework; she had wondered why the hell she couldn't have a normal mother. But now she also understood that if they found her daughter, it would be solely and exclusively because she didn't have a normal mother. She prayed every day that it would be so. Consuelo and Gloria prayed at the cross in the living room; Gloria usually held her daughter's little shoe, and Consuelo held her rosary as the two prayed in unison with the same burning desire for the girl to appear. Sometimes Ana María would join them and the voices of the three women would mingle in their entreaties for the girl to be returned to them safe and sound. The experience of maternity each woman had lived made them equals, and the aspect of her mother that had previously weighed so heavily on Gloria had been flipped around: now, it kept her afloat. Ana María had just told her over the phone that they were going to find little Gloria one way or another, and whenever she spoke with that kind of determination, her words made it so.

8.

AGUSTINA MENDÍA, MOTHER TO MARTÍN FERNÁNDEZ, felt the room spin when her son showed her the adoption papers that officially declared little Agustina Fernández Valencia to be her granddaughter. Her desire for the grandson that never materialized had been like trying to catch wind in her hands, and the wait had expanded the space and time she needed from her son. Of course she enjoyed having a granddaughter, it was good to have a granddaughter, but why was she jealous? She never said anything about her feelings explicitly, but she did make passing comments to her son like, "you didn't throw so many tantrums at that age," and "you weren't such a picky eater," or "maybe one day she'll resemble you in something." The bonds of blood that joined mother and son—solid, unbreakable, unconditional—seemed even stronger now that there was an adopted three-year-old granddaughter in the picture. A granddaughter who, moreover, bore her name.

Nuria's parents met the girl right away; Martín's mother waited two months. To be fair, her daughter-in-law wasn't exactly Agustina Mendía's favorite person. Nuria knew that her mother-in-law wasn't fond of her; she was also aware of the remarks the woman made to her husband behind her back about shortcomings in her housework. The fact is that Nuria was polite to her mother-in-law and even more considerate to her than she was to her own parents, as if she were trying to melt ice—that hardest state of water is also the nature of some people—with small gestures. Nuria actually felt a certain tenderness toward her mother-in-law and would gladly care for her if she ever fell ill, though she was almost positive that the reverse was not true. And yet, even though Nuria genuinely cared for her mother-in-law, her kind gestures were also a way she had discovered of protecting herself. Martín didn't talk about any of this with either his mother or his wife. Nuria's parents, in contrast, were a safe space for her and Martín.

The birth of Martín's paternal instinct had been a surprise for Nuria. A sense of responsibility appeared in him that she had never seen before, a sense of home he had never shown in all the years they had been married, not until his desire to be a father was realized. The joy that Agustina's arrival brought Nuria was double: on one hand, she was so happy—what had she done to deserve such luck, she wondered, in love with the moments that made up her present as she put the girl to bed, smelled her hair, looked into her eyes, watched her blinking grow slower and slower as she drifted off—and on the other, suddenly discovering Martín's tender side.

Had anyone asked Nuria before Agustina's adoption how she thought her husband was going to react, she would have said that Martín was going to leave the child's daily care to her, but something softened in his character. It was as if his sharp edges had suddenly been rounded out, a side effect she never in her wildest dreams could have anticipated. It turned out that Martín enjoyed spending time with his daughter; he enjoyed taking care of her. Moreover, he enjoyed sharing that experience with Nuria. His mother didn't want him doing things that, in her opinion, were Nuria's responsibility. Why didn't he let Nuria bathe her and change her diapers? Why the hell should her son be washing cloth diapers stained with urine and worse? But what was it, really, that bothered his mother so much? Why was she competing with a little girl, her own granddaughter?

Nuria noticed the change in Martín on the second night Agustina slept in their home; it was chilly, and he left the water running until it was warm so the girl would be more comfortable when he washed her face. Nuria would never have predicted that gesture. What had Agustina stirred in him? Nuria suddenly felt she didn't really know her husband. But isn't it better not to really know someone? What's more, isn't it better not to really know yourself?

Martín's father had left his mother for a woman ten years younger than her a few months before Martín turned three. As an adult, he didn't have a single memory of his father at home. He had never lived with any man, much less his own father. He had four photographs of him and his father and a handful of memories in parks and at traveling fairs, one trip to the circus, images altered by the passage of time. He had gone to Chapultepec Park with him once and rowed in the lake; they had visited the Three Wise Men at the Alameda and had even gone all the way to Oaxaca to see the millennia-old Árbol de Tule. It was the only trip they ever took together. Martín had been ten years old, or had he already turned eleven? Those were three of the four photographs he had with his father. When he was still a little boy, he'd think about him, and those images would seem to be made of gold; as he got older, he would be left with traces of gold on his fingers whenever he got close to those images, and they continued to lose their shine until one day they were revealed as the meager tin they were. When all was said and done, those few outings were nothing compared to the care his mother had offered without fail every single day of his thirty-seven years.

Martín never knew what it was like to sleep in the same house as his father. He had slept in the same room as him once, in separate twin-sized beds, the time they went to Oaxaca to see the tree—that huge, magnificent ahuehuete, so different from the spindly trunk that connected them as father and son, a relationship that would soon snap like a stick. But the first nights that Agustina slept at home, he felt as if he was making peace with that earlier war. His eternal childhood fantasy, his perennial desire to have a father, was satisfied in a different form by the present. He understood without words. Maybe like the way an animal senses by instinct, through its skin, by scent, Martín knew that he could give Agustina something he had longed for as a boy. He wanted to be the exact opposite of his own father. He wanted to take care of her in a thousand small ways, like letting the water run until it warmed up enough not to chill her little hands when she washed them; in doing that, in that small act, the entire universe clicked into place. How was it possible that he, who had grown up without a father, could slip so naturally into fatherhood, like how we do the unthinkable in our dreams with ease? As simple as it is to fly in a dream, that's how simple it was to be a good father. Effortless. He was prepared, he thought, for his daughter to see him as a meddler, the kind of father who would jump into a photograph uninvited, who would make father-daughter plans with her, including a special meal every Friday—who would do for her, in other words, everything he never got to experience. To let the pendulum swing all the way. The truth was, he was glad Agustina had come into their lives. He was glad she was there to fill the void left by his father, to give him the chance to be a good father to her and a good husband to Nuria. Both he and Nuria

understood this without words. More or less the way we understand gravity without knowing the theory. Nuria saw the apple
drop from the tree; it was nothing Martín could explain like a
professor in front of a blackboard, even if he had wanted to, but
there it was. He was more present than ever for Nuria and their
daughter. But that wasn't the only apple to fall during those first
weeks with Agustina.

He had no idea how this worked, or how he was going to keep
it going. He had been cast into paternity as if someone had shoved
him onstage—he, who had spent so long eating popcorn in the
audience as a son—but he was ready to assume this long-desired
role. Sometimes he felt afraid. Would he be able to be a good father? Would he be able to support his family? And what if something went wrong, what if a sudden ailment left him bedridden?
Or, worse: what if his own father's spirit took him over? What if
he discovered one day that he couldn't finish what he started?

As a teenager, Martín had confronted his mother about his
father's absence: several times with veiled remarks, a few times
sharply, and once he really laid into her. Later, he felt guilty for
having wounded her with his words; this guilt in turn wounded
him, as is so often the case. His mother was able to support him
with the money she made; she was considered an older mother at
the time, having given birth to him at thirty-five, and she raised
him all on her own. By forty, she already had gray hair and wrin-
kles, and she dressed like a woman twenty years her senior. She
took her five-year-old son everywhere with her—she worked hard
to provide for him and would have cut off her arm to give him
whatever he needed. The child was her accomplice and her com-
panion. How had he turned into that young man who judged her
so harshly? At sixteen years old, could he really believe that it
had been her fault his father had run off with a younger woman?

Martín knew that he was the center of his mother's universe; perhaps that was why he allowed himself to be so cruel to her. She felt guilty that he had grown up without a nuclear family, and that was exactly the weapon he used against her. Agustina had sunk into a chair at the breakfast table and covered her face with her hands as she wept in front of her teenage son, offering him one of her moments of greatest vulnerability.

Martín's father, who was also named Martín Fernández, had started another family; he had three children with the woman ten years younger than him, and they lived in Michoacán. Martín didn't know exactly where. The few times Martín had called him as an adult, his father had refused to see him and hung up. It also hurt Martín to know that his father had named the only boy of this new family Martín as well; maybe this was why his first impulse had been to adopt a boy and give him the same name, to teach his father a lesson about how sons should be raised. Nonetheless, if anything brought Martín joy, it was coming home early from the cinema to spend time with his little Agustina. He wanted to share that with his mother; he wanted her to be involved in his new life as a father, but it took Agustina Mendía a while to accept the presence of the family's newest member.

Agustina Mendía had been skilled at administrating the household economy. She had managed to save a good portion of the money she made as a social worker, in part because her son always attended public schools and his medical care was also covered by her employer. She had taken full advantage of the opportunities that came with being a government employee: she had a pension, medical insurance, and a mortgage on a house in Xochimilco, as well as a storefront in the same area and a car. She was the only person in her family to own one. Agustina Mendía usually visited her son and daughter-in-law, but on the few occasions Nuria went to her house she was always struck by the fact that her mother-in-law kept dolls—the kind little girls play with—in the living and dining rooms. There was a life-sized baby made of porcelain with its legs spread; the most expensive doll in the house, it had human hair and curly lashes over big glass eyes fixed on a distant horizon, and it sat on the dining room table next to the fruit bowl; there were also many common dolls made of rags or ceramics sitting on handmade doilies among the plates in the tall glass sideboard, which made Nuria feel as if she were in her mother-in-law's bedroom rather than her dining room, as if just by visiting she were invading her privacy. Martín had once explained to her that Agustina had grown up in a poor household and that she had never had dolls as a little girl, though she had desperately wanted one, so now that she was older, she bought herself a doll whenever the chance presented itself; knowing how much she liked them, Martín himself had even given her a couple of the dolls that now decorated her home. On one occasion, early on in his relationship with Nuria and long before little Agustina would appear in their lives, a shop attendant had told him that she hoped his daughter enjoyed her new doll.

When the three gathered for a meal, Martín's mother usually spoke only to him. It wasn't that she never talked to Nuria—they chatted sometimes, and even occasionally laughed—but she tended to address her son. By now it's probably clear that she was a cold woman, but I haven't mentioned her beautiful voice: Agustina Mendía sang like an angel. In the car, there was a tacit agreement between mother and son that Martín would drive and Agustina would sit in the passenger seat; if Nuria was with them, she would sit in the back. When Agustina went into the city to meet her granddaughter at the home of her son and his wife, she brought an old doll from home for the little girl, which seemed strange to

Martín. At the very least, she could have bought something new, a new doll, as a first gift to her granddaughter. During her visit, she paid more attention to her son than to the little girl, who received from her just a few pats on the back as if they were fellow judges greeting one another at court.

Martín had gotten a bit angry with his mother that day. "Why don't you try spending time with your granddaughter," he said. He wanted to share the joy of his daughter's arrival after everything they had been through. Couldn't she see that? "At least," he said, "you could sing her a song. You like to sing, and you're so good at it." This was true. Agustina Mendía had only one friend—a woman she had known since childhood and called her comadre—and she barely ever laughed, covering her teeth when she did. She was a serious woman, but no one could sing a bolero like her. Her whole expression changed when she sang. She was transformed. It was her weakness, the only space where she could release all the feelings she kept pent up inside her and channel them into her gift. Agustina Mendía, who at first glance seemed so rigid, put everything into her music and it brought joy to anyone lucky enough to hear her sing. Her comadre once suggested that she try to make a career of it, saying that her voice was just as beautiful as any of the best singers back then. Her comadre was certain that she could be as famous as any of them if she applied herself, but Agustina had told her several times that she would rather die than sing in public.

To Martín and Nuria's surprise, his mother began to sing to the child. The girl was delighted and waved her dimpled little hands and her dimpled little fingers, dancing along to the melody of that beautiful voice and its sad songs. How could Agustina Mendía sing like a goddess? It was as if all the heartbreak, all the sadness, all the pain and grief of the whole world existed for the sole purpose of being sung by such an exquisite voice. From this first encounter with her grandmother, little Agustina took a new, melodious phrase: "Arráncame la vida," which she sang badly, hitting the *r* too hard, waving her little arms, laughing.

9.

IT HAD BEEN SEVERAL WEEKS SINCE THE GLORIA MI-
randa Felipe case crossed the northern border. The search continued in the United States, and police in New York City detained
Mrs. Catherine Richardson, fifty-three years of age and born
in France, with her three children. A United States citizen, she
was the only foreign suspect in the case; she had lived above the
Miranda Felipe family in La Mascota in Colonia Juárez and had
abandoned the residence quite suddenly the day after the girl
was kidnapped. Two Poems had shared this information with
the agent he spoke to about the case early in his investigation.
That was six months ago. On the day she was arrested, Catherine
Richardson, a widow, had called her sister in New Jersey to pick
up her children, who were being held in a New York City police
station. When had she seen the girl last? Why had she left her
apartment so abruptly? Did she have any information regarding
the whereabouts of young Gloria Miranda Felipe? Mrs. Gloria
Felipe prayed to God that she did—clutching the little shoe that
she always kept close when receiving updates about the investigation, holding on to her daughter—as she listened to Rubén
Darío Hernández, who was standing next to Córdova with his
arms crossed. The arrest might lead to clues, though given that

Catherine had barely ever interacted with Gloria's daughter made her doubt that the woman knew anything. It was a feeling based more on intuition than on hope, because she wanted—no, she needed—to believe otherwise, but something told her that Catherine had no information to share. But why the hell had she run like that, the very next day? Why had she abandoned her home, leaving all her things behind? Why hadn't she moved the way everyone else does? Before he left, the reporter José Córdova gently reminded Gloria Felipe that her statement to the police, which was also published in the newspaper on the day of the kidnapping, had described the girl's shoe as brown, not black like the one she was holding. With that, he left to draft the piece that would appear in the morning edition.

It was just as Gloria Felipe and Córdova had suspected. Gloria recounted to Ana María what Captain Rubén Darío Hernández had told them: Catherine Richardson had abandoned her life in Mexico from one moment to the next and gone to the south of France, where her mother lived, because she was afraid her own children would be kidnapped. She was convinced that leaving for France would guarantee their safety and had traveled with them by boat, taking only one suitcase. She was raising them alone; a sudden illness had taken her Mexican husband over the course of one rainy month, and staying there had meant being able to raise three children on the pension she received after his death. She had even been able to write poetry and paint—still lifes and poems about absence—but she had felt compelled to leave everything behind when she turned on the radio and heard about the kidnapping of a little girl she had seen playing with one of her own children. What guaranteed her children's safety there? What if the kidnapper already had his eye on one of them?

The impact of Gloria Miranda Felipe's kidnapping was impossible to measure. The fact that the authorities still had no information after six months only heightened the fear that plagued hundreds of families around the nation. In Zapopan, Jalisco, a group of women prayed every Saturday at an afternoon mass held in her honor; in Monterrey, a ten-year-old girl had been moved to search for little Gloria by going door-to-door; in the Purépecha lands of Michoacán state, from Uruapan to Cherán, communities had organized themselves—a family that made musical instruments in Paracho, potters in Patamban, people who specialized in building traditional wooden trojes around San Juan Parangaricutirimícuaro, forest protectors and collectors of honey, mushrooms, and wood in Cherán, as well as artisans in Uruapan—to gather part of their earnings to supplement the reward offered by Ana María; they were also organizing a pilgrimage, during which they would carry a banner embroidered with a prayer for the girl, to deliver the money to the Miranda Felipe family in Mexico City.

The gestures of solidarity that the family received came from places they had never imagined, and several of them made Gloria Felipe cry, especially the offering from Michoacán, the state where Consuelo grew up and where her parents were taking care of her daughter, Alicia. The Miranda Felipe family had gone to Tlalpujahua de Rayón a couple of times over the years, to Alicia's First Communion and to the Mass and celebration honoring the golden anniversary of Consuelo's parents. That prayer embroidered with the name of her daughter had moved Gloria Felipe even more because she knew the kindness behind the support being offered—it was the same kindness she saw in Consuelo when she played with her children. Goodness did exist. Goodness existed in the way Consuelo sang rancheras to her sons and taught them how to sing along, the same goodness Consuelo showed when she helped them find the right notes, or when she bathed them every day, even though she was so far from Alicia, the daughter she never got to raise, and whom she had sung to and bathed only a few times. Goodness did exist, but so did the evil that kept her from her daughter.

The only sound Gloria Felipe heard was her daughter's name; it was as if Gustavo, Luis, Jesús, and Carlos had collectively slipped down to a second tier. They had received so many letters and calls from complete strangers, all those expressions of support radiating like the concentric circles that form when a stone is cast into still water. These stories moved Gloria as if they were gifts themselves, but at the same time they were unnecessary gifts: the only thing she wanted was the one thing she didn't have, and she felt an emptiness nothing could fill. As the days passed and the reward increased, the number of fake kidnappers also grew, with their fake stories that piled up like a heap of useless waste. All they did was sully the air in her home, perhaps to remind her that the only thing she wanted was the one thing she didn't have. Nothing could satisfy Gloria, not until her daughter came home.

On one of those afternoons, Gloria stopped speaking. She didn't answer her husband or her children; she spent hours staring out the window until the indecipherable voice of her husband sent her into the bathroom carrying an ashtray that she proceeded spend a long time cleaning with a cloth she had taken from the cabinet, behind the locked door, despite the fact that the ashtray was already spotless.

It took a lot to get to this point, but—as if the shoe that her daughter had mistakenly clung to thinking it was little Gloria's was the drop that made the bucket spill over—the day after her daughter told her about the arrest of Catherine Richardson, Ana María decided to use the ace up her sleeve: she would go to see a bruja known as La Jefa, who worked with politicians and many of Ana María's own clients. Several had mentioned La Jefa but Ana María had always seen their accounts as charming curiosities, or at most interesting anecdotes, because she was Catholic and because she had a hard time believing what she heard: that La Jefa could grant any wish, to the letter. There was still a part of her that doubted. She herself had the gift of being able to say whether a pregnant client was going to have a boy or a girl with the help of a cross on a delicate chain she always carried with her, which spun one way or the other; in those days before ultrasounds, many women had gone to see her. She had always been right; she had always guessed whether the baby would be a boy or a girl. What if that were possible on a bigger scale? What if this woman could guess more than the answer to a simple question; what if she could see more complex things? What if she could provide clues about her granddaughter?

Dressed elegantly, as always, Ana María arrived at a single-story brick house with two windows in the front and a room with no windows in the back. A teenage girl with a child's face and large breasts opened the chain-link fence and led her to that windowless room, saying that her grandmother would be right with her. There were dogs, roosters, hens running loose, pigs in a corral, and an owl in a cage over which an old, ripped sweater hung like a threadbare cupola. Along the way, Ana María caught scents so different from what she was used to in the city that they stood out even more: animal waste, tortillas drying on a board in the sun, wood burning in a stove, beans cooking in a clay pot, herbs, fat, urine, dry earth, more feces under the hot sun. Once inside the room, Ana María looked at the collection of different sized candles in one corner, a few of which were lit. She noticed how dark the room was, the staleness of the air, and the different fresh herbs separated into little heaps on the table. As her eyes fell on the chipped rays emanating from the head of a Virgin of Guadalupe, she heard a voice behind her. The woman asked Ana María to place her purse, hat, and gloves on a cot in the corner; meanwhile, she moved the herbs from the table to a corner of the dirt floor. She brought a candle over to the table, pulled a deck of Spanish cards from her apron, and asked Ana María to sit facing her. She needed to do a reading before they could begin.

This is what La Jefa said to Ana María:

"All right, let's see now, mija. I can't see if you came from hardship before in your family, but what I do see is that you shine; just like the stars, you shine in your family against the dark. People see you from far away. Look, here you are. But this card tells me that something is missing, something more important that the coins you earned. This card tells me that coins give you stability; many times has God said to you, here you go, take these coins, mija, but that's not what he is saying to you now about the thing that brought you here. I can see it, it's getting clearer, you're here because of your family, that's what this card here says, your coins have no value in this. Do you see it? We're going to ask the cards. All right, I'll tell you. It says here that your family is fine, but you're facing a storm. Look, here are the clubs raining down hard like a storm on your family. See it? Like the storms that follow a black frost, the kind that leaves the whole field burnt and black. But look here, you have blessings, here it says you have blessings you brought upon yourself, look at all the coins, all these coins here tell me you made your fortune and with it you can begin to regrow after the black frost. And why not, mija. But here I see something you couldn't do, here it says you're stuck and can't see the harvest after the black frost because of something here. Here

96

it says you can't save the whole world, you have to save your own world first."

The teenage girl with a child's face and large breasts interrupted to ask if she should kill a chicken that day or the next. The woman stepped out briefly to give her instructions for the chicken soup and returned to the table with Ana María, remarking how well her daughter made the dish, but she wasn't there at the moment, so her granddaughter would be making lunch. She was about to say something else about the food when she saw the horrified look on Ana María's face and focused on the cards.

"You can't save the whole world, mija, because first you have to save your world, that's what the cards say, that's what they say right here, God as my witness. We can't help anyone unless we help ourselves. Nobody can. That's why you're stuck: you save one, you save another, but first save you, 'cause if you don't, nobody will. Nobody will save you, mija. That's just how it is. Pick three cards, mija. Aha, look here, the other shoe. You've always got your angle. The cards say the storm is getting worse and bringing with it even the black frost because you're always looking for an angle. You don't do anything without thinking of how it could benefit you. You always look for profit, always need to hear God saying, take these coins, mija. You see what I mean? How did you manage to only look at others and never at yourself all this time? Let's see, pick seven cards. Listen, you can't see anything if the thing you're looking for on the outside is something you can't see on the inside. And here it says you don't want to see it. Right here, you see? So tell me, mija. Your granddaughter. Two and a half years old. Six months? You want to know where she's been these past six months. All right, let's see, mija, pick seven cards. Would you believe what the cards are telling me? You can't worship a saint you don't see. But the saint is right there, whether you see him or not. Just because you can't see him doesn't mean he's not there, you see? Just because you can't see her doesn't mean you can't worship her. Your granddaughter is there in that suit of cups, there she is, do you see her? Here she is. Just like my granddaughter is there at the hearth, we can't see either of them, but there they are, you see? Tell me your granddaughter's full name and put both hands on the cards. Now close your eyes and pick three cards. Mija, you're going to have to figure that one out yourself, I can't tell you that, but here we are, I'm seeing it right here, by God's will. You need to see it, too, mija. I'll put you in a circle of fire. Go stand over by the cot."

La Jefa made a ring of salt around Ana María, who was now standing in the middle of the room, and began to whisper prayers in a different language, one Ana María did not recognize. The teenage girl with a child's face opened the door again with a wooden spoon in her hand, but this time, when she saw Ana María inside the salt circle, she withdrew without interrupting them. La Jefa splashed alcohol mixed with herbs onto the circle and told Ana María that she was going to set fire to the salt in order to see her granddaughter. Ana María began to feel the heat and to hear the salt crackling in the fire around her. The flames stayed low to the ground. Ana María didn't know what to do with her arms, her feet. She felt the fire's heat and heard the crackle of the salt. La Jefa asked her to close her eyes and stay very still. She began to speak in another language, braiding it with words in Spanish like braiding long hair: the Lord's Prayer, a few words in another language, another Lord's Prayer, another sentence in what seemed to be that other language, another Lord's Prayer. Ana María opened her eyes and peeked across the fire in the faint light that entered through the crack under the door, and she heard a rooster crow in the background and the barking of dogs in the distance, and she managed to beg the woman to please, please help find her granddaughter.

"You lost two sons," said La Jefa to Ana María. "Here they are," she said, "close your eyes."

And those unexpected words were like a key that had not been turned in her since she lost them on the cement floor of a rooftop storage room, bleeding, realizing that they were two and not one, that their genitals had formed and they were two boys, two boys that were perfect even though they were so small, too small, and one of them was smiling while the other was not, as if to mark their personalities with that one simple difference; it was an image Ana María had not seen since she was twenty-eight years old, as if she had buried that image in a black trunk but it suddenly came rushing back, along with the feeling of her backside freezing against the concrete floor, the intense pain, and the smell of iron coming from her blood, all that blood, when she saw the smile of her tiny baby, a baby that was at once hers and not hers, that was hers and also of another world, that other world, that world that made this one different, that made this a terrible world in which those two babies never opened their eyes, this different world in which she held in her hands a fully formed but far too small baby who would never open his eyes, trying on a smile, and when she saw that smile she began to cry. La Jefa fueled the fire with more alcohol and with that heat, which was so different from the cold of the concrete on the roof where she had lost her twins, Ana María lost control and wept over everything, including her own birth.

La Jefa prayed in Spanish until Ana María was able to breathe steadily again. "You left your pain here, mija," she told her. "Fire cleans deeper than water. Now, mija, now you're truly clean. Now you can see your granddaughter because you put your boys away in your heart, they're not in your fears anymore. Your granddaughter," she said, "I don't know where she is, the cards won't tell me and the fire, neither, but what they do tell me is you'll find her before six moons have passed, the darkness hides her from me but before six moons have passed you'll find her because she's right there. The last moon will guide you."

The fire that encircled Ana María was about to go out, and La Jefa controlled it with a few mouthfuls of water that she spat on the flames. She said the Lord's Prayer again and dropped a fistful of the burnt salt in a little muslin bag that she tied with a red string as she told Ana María that the fire of her loss would light the way to her granddaughter. She told her to place the little bag of salt under her pillow, and that everything she needed to know would come to her in a dream. Ana María paid ten times the price they had agreed on, and the teenage girl met them on their way to the chain-link gate to offer her ripe capulin cherries from a metal bucket and invite her to stay for lunch, but she thanked the girl quickly, gave her more money, and went home.

That night, Ana María was struck by insomnia and the vision of her twins that had visited her earlier was just as vivid more than thirty years later, as if she had lost the pregnancy that day. As if, emotionally speaking, her pain had frozen time and not a second had passed between that moment and this one. She was twenty-eight and almost sixty in a single instant. The smell of her blood, the weight of her fully developed but tiny babies, so small and light and perfect—the pain, always imperfect—pushing them out on that cracked cement floor, its cold seeping into her. What had made her burst into tears with La Jefa had been remembering the names she had come up with for her sons on the day she lost them; she had decided to name them right there, to give them some weight in this world, the weight of their names not attached to any past or future tense but always in the present, and as she thought about those names that were just as present as they had been back then, as if she had spent years hiding them from herself, those names she had never revealed to anyone, she fell asleep just before dawn.

Ana María slept for an hour. She dreamed about the hot springs she used to visit with her father not long before he died, though in her dream she was around fifty years old; in this impossible scene, she and her father were having a conversation about different types of paella. She awoke with the vivid sensation that she had just been with her father, talking about paella, and that he had been able to hear her without any trouble, after not seeing him since she was thirteen years old, talking about something she had never really thought about, but why would her father return from the Great Beyond to talk to her about paella and tell her that the best spicy sausage he ever tasted was in a little town in Andalucía. With pounding head and puffy eyes, still in the fog of a conversation that had ended with the best spicy sausage her father ever tasted, she called Beatriz and asked her to attend to the first clients scheduled that morning, while with her other hand she held the little bag of salt.

She didn't say a word about her visit with La Jefa to her daughter or son-in-law, but she did call Captain Rubén Darío Hernández to ask for an update on the search. She was inclined to pester him constantly from then on, to call him three times a day and add more money to the pot if it meant not losing her granddaughter, unlike the sons she did lose. No, she was not inclined to see her granddaughter dead like she had seen her sons, whose names she would hold until her very last breath.

10.

IT HAD BEEN SIX MONTHS SINCE LITTLE GLORIA'S kidnapping, and the Miranda Felipe family still knew nothing about her whereabouts. As a couple, Gloria and Gustavo rarely had spats or arguments, but when they did fight, it was like Troy burning to the ground.

That day, the argument began when their son Jesús asked permission to spend the following weekend with a friend from school. His father said yes, but Gloria didn't want her son sleeping in someone else's home. That was how it started. Jesús left his parents fighting in their room, and the blaze grew: Gustavo insinuated that it was Gloria's fault their daughter had been kidnapped—how could she leave her with a stranger, what the hell was she thinking—and Gloria blamed her husband for not doing anything to find her, saying that it was her mother pulling all the strings. They went back and forth, wounding each other more deeply with every indictment, and the fire spread, consuming their room and lapping at the entire house.

The fight escalated until Gustavo fell silent and refused to respond, which was his way of manipulating his wife. Furious, he didn't speak to her for several days, during which she expressed her dissatisfaction with him through their children—her preferred form of manipulation. They couldn't stand each other. They avoided being in the same room and whenever they did end up in the same place it was awful to be around them. Had Gustavo been a bit more daring, he would have left home for a few days, until the cloud of dust that made it so hard to breathe had cleared. But where would he go? To Ana María's house? She was like a mother to him; he had lost his own parents years earlier, and his wife and their family was all he had. The moment the thought crossed his mind, it seemed unnecessary—impossible, even—to leave his family. His four sons were keenly aware that they were of secondary importance to their mother, a supporting cast as long as the star was missing, and he had been distant from them, too, these past few days. They hadn't ceased to exist for him; quite the contrary: he was there for them like he always was, but he had fought with his wife and felt distant from himself, as if he were watching his own life through a pane of glass. Tavo saw the tension between his parents and tried to reconcile them; for the time being, he took care of his little brothers while his parents sent each other messages through him.

They usually enjoyed their little spats, but this fight had wounded them more deeply than any before. It's true that they were in the worst situation they had ever experienced, one they wouldn't have imagined in their most horrifying nightmares. Both had thought of leaving their home, their family, the whole situation, as if all of it could be stuffed into a heavy-duty trash bag and brought to the dump. Carlos began wetting his school uniform and using expletives he didn't entirely understand the meaning of, as if he wanted to seem older at the same time he was soiling himself like a baby. Consuelo washed his clothes, saving him a tongue lashing from his father, and probably a belt lashing, too—as much as he loved them, Gustavo hit his sons to teach them their lessons, as was common once. Especially for a man raising sons, just like he had been raised. Gustavo the father was ill-tempered: little things would send him into a fury. He had no sense of scale, every issue was major, and Gloria had no desire to see him or speak with him. She was lonely; if they agreed on one thing, it was that they both felt lonely. And something else: each thought the other was wrong. They fought about everything, attacking and defending. As a matter of fact, Gloria Felipe and Gustavo Miranda had gotten into an argument when they met.

It was at a holiday party. She was fifteen; he was twenty-one and found her attractive. What was it about her eyes that made him feel so comfortable, as if he were in the coziest corner of his home, as if he already knew her? What was it he liked so much about the melodic way she spoke, the way she peppered her conversations with laughter? She wasn't even talking to him, she was talking to another girl, but right there, in line for punch, he said to her, crossing his arms, that he knew her from somewhere. Gloria knew it wasn't true—she had never seen this thin young man with a sharp nose and a crisp side part in his hair before—but she was charmed by the way he had approached her, so she made a passing remark about the party. They argued about the lyrics of a villancico as they approached the punch bowl. Gloria was certain that the song said one thing, Gustavo insisted that it said another, and they laughed and flirted as they argued, though each was certain the other was wrong. The first few times they went out together, Ana María sent her mother as a chaperone, and both Ana María and her mother remarked at different times how much the young couple liked to argue. They enjoyed making jokes about them afterward, reenacting their disputes; Ana María's mother observed at one point that they were more like street pigeons than turtledoves, bickering over crumbs that neither would eat.

Their connection had been based on arguing, ever since the day they met. On the other hand, they also had great conversations, over long afternoons that turned into years. Like a single fire, the flames of conversing and arguing rose to the same height.

A friend of Gloria's from high school was about to get married. Gloria and Gustavo had been together for years and she thought it was a good time to discuss taking their relationship to the next level. Gustavo wasn't sure he was ready yet. He needed more economic stability in order to keep her in the lifestyle she was used to with Ana María. The bar was set high. Gloria invited Gustavo to her friend's wedding, and that fact started an argument that went back and forth between going to the wedding and getting married, which led to Gustavo's impulsive decision to distance himself from Gloria. They had never slept together, both had their beliefs in that regard; he felt they didn't owe each other anything and that going their separate ways would be the best thing for them both. So they didn't speak for five months. Gloria was a proud woman and, though she missed him, she was certain that sooner or later they would be reunited. Then a friend told her that she had seen Gustavo strolling through the park, holding hands with another girl. Gloria didn't want to hear any more. Her grandmother said she shouldn't even think about contacting him. "You deserve to choose," she said, "don't wait around to be chosen." The news about Gustavo pained Gloria, and she spent entire nights thinking about him holding another girl's hand. She imagined a thousand and one scenes of the life they could have shared. During her nights of insomnia, she chided herself for not having done things differently with him, for not having said different things, but one morning she decided to let him go. "Let your light shine, my dear, and they'll be on you like moths to a flame," Gloria's grandmother told her over a breakfast of pastries one day. And that's precisely what happened: that morning, Gloria relaxed. She let him go. She had always wanted to learn how to cut and style hair, so she began spending all her free time at the salon, experimenting with elaborate styles that the salon's clientele started requesting more and more often. Many clients commented to Ana María and her mother how lovely and attentive Gloria was, and one of them even told Gloria, while she was doing her hair, that she wanted to introduce her to her son and would invite her over the first chance she got.

Nearly five months after they stopped speaking, and only a few days before the party where the client planned to introduce Gloria to her son, Gustavo sought her out to tell her that he missed her and wanted to be with her. He knew that getting back together would mean getting married, so he went ahead and proposed. At the end of the day, he felt he'd never find anyone he enjoyed talking with as much as he did with her, and on top of that, she was attractive. The fact of the matter is that he was head over heels for Gloria. He wanted to start a family with her and remain close with Ana María, who had always been so supportive of him. Gloria enjoyed talking with him, too. She loved him. Not long after they got back together, Gustavo asked Ana María and Gloria's grandmother for her hand in marriage. "Such wonderful news," Ana María exclaimed. "It's about time to move on from that very long engagement. I'll pay for the wedding." That day, she also called him "son" for the first time, not realizing how much it meant to him.

A week before her daughter's wedding, Ana María's mother told her that she wished she hadn't gotten divorced, so Gloria could walk down the aisle on her father's arm, rather than her mother's. In her mind, divorce was a sin. "It's your cross to bear," she had said when Ana María told her about the divorce, just like she had said when the Spaniard whose name we will not speak gave her daughter a venereal disease after sleeping with someone—Ana María never knew who or where—when Gloria was still a baby. She also told Ana María it was her cross to bear when she complained to her mother that he came home drunk and mistreated her, shouted at her; she offered another "it's your cross to bear" when he beat her until Ana María lost the twins. After everything she had been through, thought Ana María, it was fine if Gloria and Gustavo argued, that was just their personalities; they wanted to be together, and she could tell that Gustavo had a good heart, which was all she cared about, especially in the man who would be making a life with her daughter. Their union also seemed like good news for her, as if the universe were offering her a chance, in the form of her son-in-law, to make peace with men after so many years of lumping them all together. She had struggled since the divorce, shying away from any kind of intimacy. Yet here was this committed, upstanding young man without vices or the need to prove his masculinity through violence, unlike that Spaniard whose name we will not mention. Ana María was certain he would be an excellent father to her grandchildren; when those grandchildren arrived, Gustavo surpassed all expectations. He was involved in raising them and enjoyed taking care of them. He loved being a father and had a tender side.

Gustavo Miranda and Gloria Felipe were married on October 22, 1933. After their first dance as bride and groom, Gustavo asked the band to play the villancico they had heard at the holiday party where they met. With the song still going in the background, he told the story of his first encounter with Gloria and said a few loving words to her; while the guests applauded, the band struck up a song for dancing. Ana María, moved and happy, broke the ice, dancing with Gustavo while Gloria danced with her grandmother, which was unusual for the time. Ana María was also the last to leave the dance floor that night. She chatted with everyone who joined her out there, celebrating her daughter and son-in-law, having a blast. It was a joyous day for the couple, but also and especially for Ana María, who not only had a great time but also reconciled herself with her past, as if her daughter's wedding were a new moon, a celebration of life and joy, everything her marriage with the Spaniard—whose name we will not speak—failed to give her. Not even at her own wedding had she enjoyed herself as much.

Photographs from the wedding appeared in magazines and the society pages of several newspapers. Gloria's grandmother, the family's unofficial archivist, had made clippings of everything related to that day, and Gloria saved those in a box along with other loose pictures and family albums inside a wooden chest she kept in her closet, which had been a gift from her mother after one of her trips. Made for storing clothes, it contained sheets of rose-scented paper and held not only her wedding dress, but the entire outfit she had worn to the holiday party the day she met Gustavo, including the shoes. Gustavo didn't see anything unusual about his wife saving her wedding dress, that was something married women often did, but the fact that she had saved the outfit she was wearing when they met warmed his heart each time he saw that chest in the back of the closet.

Gustavo liked his routines; he liked reading about Mexican and world history and listening to the radio, which was always tuned to the same station; he liked wearing blue or black socks—never any other colors or, God forbid, patterns—and he liked observing anniversaries of all kinds. Every year, he had a little pendant made of the material that corresponded to their wedding anniversary. Not long after he presented her with a pendant ingeniously crafted of white paper and hung from a delicate silver chain for their first anniversary, Gloria gave birth to their first child. Ana María crumbled then crumbled again, and then all those pieces crumbled with love for her grandson Tavo. Those first days with the newborn at home were happy ones. Pure and simple: they were happy days.

What would happen if they didn't find their little girl, who was by now just over two and a half years old? What would happen if they found her and she wasn't alive? They didn't dare say the word *dead*, acting like it didn't exist, just like there's no word for parents who lose a child. And what would happen if her kidnapper hurt her somehow? What would happen to the two of them? What would they do with the guilt? And what would become of her as a mother if someone had sexually abused her little girl? Done her some kind of physical harm? What would happen if they never again saw their little girl, Gloria Miranda Felipe, who weighed nine pounds and four ounces when she was born in the small hours of December 30, 1943?

One afternoon, Gloria Felipe left home and got lost somewhere. They spent hours searching for her. Gustavo was worried sick, while Ana María was certain that Gloria would turn up, though not as late that night as she did. The children never found out; Consuelo made up a story to explain their mother's absence, though she was frightened, too, and concerned about her employer. Perhaps Gloria thought that if her daughter was lost, then she deserved to be lost as well. There was no rational or medical explanation for Gloria Felipe's disappearance that afternoon.

Gloria and Gustavo were as tense as if they were dangling in midair. No one could give them any kind of guarantee, and all their efforts seemed to have been in vain. Between them, it was like looking into a dark mirror: neither could offer a reflection back to the other. Maybe, like two people trapped on a desert island without food or any chance of escape, the only way they could express to the universe that they had no idea how the hell their daughter wasn't with them was by devouring each other like cannibals in their fights.

They were in the middle of another pointless argument when the phone rang and a man's voice said, "I've seen your daughter."

11.

THAT MORNING, AS SHE SAT AT HER DESK IN THE CAR-
diologist's office, Nuria Valencia had heard on the radio that a minor had been rescued from captivity at the border with the United
States. The announcer ended his report by saying, "but we still
have no news about the girl all of Mexico is searching for." This
was enough to make Constanza stop typing and remark to Nuria
that she and her mother were beside themselves about the little
girl's kidnapping, which had made them even more nervous about
her own son, who was about to turn four. The young woman and
her mother had felt the need to take precautions out of fear that
someone would steal their "little bean," as Constanza called her
son. She asked how Nuria's family was handling those fears.

For the very first time, Nuria opened up to her colleague. She
told her how little they had taken Agustina out. She had gotten
all her vaccines; they'd taken her to the city clerk to finalize her
adoption and to her grandmother's house in Xochimilco, but that
was basically all. They hadn't even taken her to visit Nuria's parents' home in Morelos. She wasn't allowed to play in their gated
community, much less out on the street. She barely ever left the
house. They were so lucky, really, that her parents had been able

to come stay with them in the city and take care of the little girl while she and Martín were at work.

"Since our little beans are shut in all the time," said Constanza, "maybe we could make a playdate one of these days. And while we're at it, I could pass on some clothes and toys we've outgrown." This seemed like a good idea to Nuria—the offer of clothing and toys was helpful, though not indispensable, and it would have been good for Agustina to spend time with another child—but the distance she and her coworker had established long before seemed like a line drawn in chalk between their desks, like the kind drawn to indicate the edge of a stage, and there was no way Nuria was going to cross it. What did she mean, get together outside the hospital? It seemed forced, like an actor chatting with a member of the audience at the theater entrance; in this case, Nuria was the audience to her easygoing and sociable coworker. The mere thought of having a relationship with her outside the office made Nuria uncomfortable. Unlike Nuria, Constanza had an active social life with several other coworkers and, without pausing to set a date, she moved right on to how some of the other mothers at the hospital's daycare center, access to which was provided by the institution, had changed their habits as the months of Gloria Miranda Felipe's kidnapping went by, how they had practically quarantined their little beans, she said, as if they were living in a pandemic that threatened their lives each time they stepped outside.

Nuria Valencia usually kept her eyes on the ground as she walked, observing the cracks and lines of the pavement without paying much attention to her surroundings, but that day, on her way home from work, she looked up, paying attention to the streets and the parks, listening to snippets of conversations, and Constanza's words echoed everywhere. The city had been emptied

of young people, though children had been playing freely outdoors just a few months earlier. The three she saw as she walked
home were all holding hands with an adult. It was true: times
had changed. She realized that what was happening in her home
was a scaled version of what was happening in a larger reality, or
rather, on a national level. Sometimes the significance of a story
can be measured only by the impact it has, and the case of Gloria
Miranda Felipe had limited Agustina's development, just as it had
done to Constanza's son. And—Nuria intuited, she knew—to so
many other children as well. Come to think of it, Agustina had
several verbal peculiarities that made her sound like an adult. She
imitated certain formalities that Nuria's parents used, especially
her father, who was always very polite with the customers at the
hardware store; from her mother, she had gotten "beg your pardon?" and "but of course," both of which came out of her mouth
all the time, along with a use of diminutives that made her sound
more like a well-heeled granny than a little girl. To say nothing of
the heartbreaking songs she learned from her other grandmother,
whose name she shared. What effect would being shut in like this
have on young people later in life? In what direction did the isola-
tion sparked by the threat of being ripped from their families push
their development?

On her walk home that day, for the first time, Nuria seemed
to see the city from above. It was a city very different from the one
we know today, one with volcanos in the distance and air as clean
as a freshly washed sheet hung to dry under the all-illuminating
sun, and downtown neighborhoods that once represented the entire urban spread; rivers running, many maps ago, among cars,
people, and buildings, and the sun reflecting off their ripples and
mutable forms, a lake city where the smells of nature and concrete intermingled, where the stores bore different names: unique,

full names that don't exist anymore, not in photographs or in the memory of the children of the pedestrians who saw them every day; poppies in bloom on the medians along the Paseo de la Reforma; people strolling around the Zócalo on the weekend and having their photos taken. That city no longer exists, but it did once, just like a woman named Nuria Valencia existed, a woman who wondered as she walked home how many children like her daughter had been developmentally curtailed by not being allowed outside, sometimes not even to go to school, because of this public safety crisis.

The state could do nothing to stop the wave of kidnappings, and the case of Gloria Miranda Felipe was the tragic emblem of a problem that struck the nation at its heart: its children. Time had needed to pass for Nuria to fully understand that her feelings were shared by many others: the terror that someone would steal her child from her. She tried to imagine how it would be. It would be painful, she imagined. Unimaginably painful, she imagined. I can't stand to even imagine it, she thought. I should think of something else. That evening when she got home, Nuria insisted on putting her daughter to bed. Martín had been looking forward to doing it, but that night it was something Nuria needed. Martín resigned himself to the change and used the time to call his mother, who was having trouble with the landlord of her shop in Xochimilco. For some reason, the little girl was angry with her mother and called her Nuria. She had been calling her Mami, and the gesture deflated Nuria as if her daughter had a pin and Nuria were a balloon being offered to her. The little girl was beginning to understand the power she had over the emotions of her adoptive parents. Nuria didn't let on that her daughter had hurt her feelings and read *The Ugly Duckling* as her bedtime story. Agustina asked her not to stroke her hair that night, and Nuria respected her wishes. She also asked her not to touch her arm, and Nuria respected that request as well. Nuria was terrified that someone might kidnap her, that someone might rip her from their home, but it had never crossed her mind that her daughter might push them away, just like she was pushing Nuria away that night. What if the time came when Agustina wanted nothing to do with her adoptive parents?

Nuria remained a while longer in the girl's bed, wondering what Agustina remembered of her previous life, how far back her memory stretched, and what she would remember as an adult. The limits of the child's language was a single square meter that Nuria knew like the back of her hand, having followed her speech day by day; within those confines, Agustina had mentioned something about the juice she used to drink and that she had liked candies, but not much more. Was there a before and an after to being adopted in her mind? Did she remember anything? Would she later? But really: did she remember anything? What if over time, as her language grew, Agustina could recreate her entire past like an astronomer naming every star and forming a new map with this new knowledge, rejecting the little planetarium her adoptive parents had offered.

It hadn't been easy to get her to call them "Papi" and "Mami," but she did, eventually. What if she rejected the adoption as soon as she came of age? A new fear settled into Nuria. What did her daughter dream about? Were the things she dreamed about but couldn't describe things she had seen in her past life, the one she had before living with them, or were they about her present? What would Nuria do if her daughter came to resent the adoption? What if her biological father showed up out of nowhere? Or, worse, what if Agustina turned her back on them one day and closed the door on them, never to let them in again? What if she became self-destructive when she reached adolescence, throwing herself into the void of alcohol or some other vice? Doing herself harm in a fit of rage, for example, furious over not fitting in a world full of "normal" families—which today we call heteronormative— and because she didn't feel loved by her biological parents, so who could ever love her? Self-destruction. After all, if her biological parents and grandparents hadn't loved her, why should she love herself? Anything was possible: the worst nightmare was possible precisely where the greatest dream had come true. Why wasn't society made to accommodate other kinds of families, wondered Nuria, lying listless on Agustina's bed, as if these questions had cut her strings and she was just a sad, worn-out puppet tired of performing the same show over and over. But what she couldn't see was that these fears, which popped up like shadows and kept changing shapes, were simply anxiety over her lack of control. She had no control—not over what might happen to her daughter, nor over whether her daughter might want to leave home or hurt herself, nor over whether someone might try to kidnap her, taking away the happiness she and Martín had finally found. Why not trust, then? Why not trust in the love she felt for her daughter, for her husband, for her parents, for all the goodness she felt in Agustina's presence, the same goodness that was throwing the shadows a sleepless Nuria watched without the strength to rise, more terrified by the moment.

Nuria fell asleep in her daughter's bed that night, and this is what she dreamed: their landlady, a woman they had never met in person—they had only dealt with one of her sons—appeared, attentive and solemnly dressed, and walked into Nuria's living room as if they were old acquaintances. Water was seeping through the walls, revealing the pipes behind them: pipes along which water flowed like emotions. The walls appeared to be sweating. To show her landlady the damage, Nuria ran her hand over one of them and a mix of white paint, water, lime, filler, and clay remained on her hand, as if the walls were malleable, as if the house, perhaps, were alive. As if it were a living thing. And that wasn't the worst part. In Agustina's room, which wasn't inside the house in Nuria's dream—a strange detail, because why would the girl's room be anywhere but inside the house—Nuria showed the landlady how the walls wept there, too. They wept like someone releasing torrents of sadness. The water ran straight down them like a rain that does no good because so much falls at once. As if the water were keeping a secret. Nuria woke up just as she was asking the landlady how they were going to fix the problem, but before she was given an answer. It was the middle of the night. She ran a hand across Agustina's forehead, where her bangs were matted down with sweat. The little girl had grown a few new curls, perfect ringlets that Nuria brushed into place with her fingers before stroking her forehead again, whispering "I love you" into her ear, and heading for the bed she shared with Martín, who was snoring like a chainsaw.

Nuria couldn't fall asleep. She was angry at how loudly her husband was snoring, but he had always snored like that, and she had gotten used to it. Why did it bother her so much that night? Maybe she was angry with him because when you're in a relationship it's easier to cast blame on your partner than to look inside yourself. The same way, perhaps, that the opposite is also true: you can only really feel love when you direct it at someone else. What she was angry about was that Agustina had called her by her name. She was angry because her husband hadn't woken her up from her bad dream. Her bad dream had made her feel like there was a defect in her home, and not just in her home, but in her life as well, the same defect that allowed her adopted daughter to push her away by calling her by her given name. Her adopted daughter, who pushed her away by calling her by her name. That was why she was angry: because Agustina wasn't her biological daughter.

Her husband's snoring got louder; it was unbearable. It was all unbearable: her husband, her room, her bed. It was unbearable to be her. She nudged his shoulder and then changed his position, but this new position made him snore even louder to a new, more infuriating, rhythm. Nuria shouted a complaint at Martín, who responded more asleep than awake but stopped snoring. She remained angry, even after he fell silent—now it was his breathing that bothered her—maybe because getting angry at your partner is the best place to hide from your deepest fears. Anger at a romantic partner: that deafening emotion behind which all others can hide.

12.

ONE NIGHT, ANA MARÍA FELIPE WAS GETTING READY for a party and decided to wear the expensive ring she had bought herself a few days earlier, on the anniversary of the day she opened her first business with her mother. Though she didn't think of it in these terms, during those years she had changed the professional landscape in Mexico: from the tiny beauty parlor where she got her start, to her celebrated salon, multiple clothing shops, and exclusive bridal boutique, she was the first woman to reach such heights in business and the first Mexican designer to be invited to international runway shows. She had some of the world's most important fashion designers as her peers and engaged in lively conversations over the phone in English, French, and Italian, using colloquial phrases and all; she also had a large staff, many of whom were women who might not have achieved economic independence otherwise in that oppressive society. She was known for her good taste and charisma. She loved to socialize, genuinely enjoying her interactions with people, and this appreciation was more than mutual. Time seemed not only to multiply her wealth and prestige, but also to expand her influence. She was both creatively talented and professionally successful, an anomaly for a woman in the 1940s. This ring represented all that, too.

During several of the conversations she had with small groups, she played with her new ring as if her red nails were arrows pointing at the dazzling jewel. She had a lovely evening and felt more relaxed than she had in a long time; she also felt proud of being able to buy herself that ring with money she earned, doubly so, she realized at the party, because she had bought it with money she earned doing something she loved, which was in and of itself a gift—an invisible gift the other partygoers couldn't see, but that the ring reminded her of that night. A ring on those fingers that got their start playing piano in a silent movie theater, those fingers that made her dreams possible thanks to the education her father managed to provide.

She made no bones about the fact that she was one of the few people at the party able to build a comfortable life—make that a luxurious life—doing something that she loved. For Ana María, at that party, at least, the ring was a crown, and not the kind of crown that money can buy, but the crown of her freedom. After all, she had turned the dresses she dreamed up as a young woman into reality and still enjoyed working at nearly sixty years old, and those two hands that owed so much to her parents— both of whom had passed away by then—seemed to sparkle in that ring, along with everything she herself had achieved since she played piano in that silent movie theater. Ana María joined a conversation solely because the group was standing near a lamp and she wanted the light to play off her ring. A woman in the circle asked how the search for her granddaughter was going, and Ana María replied candidly about the investigation, as if she had known her for a long time. Why did she feel so light when talking about a topic that had felt so heavy before? Could it be a sign that everything was or was going to be all right? What was happening? She didn't know, but this peaceful sensation allowed her to enjoy the party. That evening, a man followed her from group to group, wanting to ask her to dinner, wanting to get to know her. A fabric manufacturer three years her junior who had two children and a granddaughter and was drawn to Ana María like a magnet.

She returned home in the small hours of the morning slightly tipsy after dancing and enjoying herself all night. Still, she removed her cosmetics and prepared herself for bed as she did every night because no matter what time she got home she never rushed through taking off her makeup and putting on her pajamas. Ana María donned a silk nightgown that she kept on the side of her closet designed especially for her furs. Having decided to leave her ring on the nightstand as if its diamonds could watch over her sleep like the eyes of wolves, she had a vivid dream that she was traveling—in Italy, perhaps. She didn't recognize the place, it seemed like a bricolage with certain traits from here and there, a collage city with canals like Venice, a cathedral like the one in Milan outside of which she had fed pigeons, a restaurant where she had dined in Cuernavaca, and a corner from Colonia Polanco, where she had one of her shops. The opposite corner was identical to one she had visited a long time ago with her mother and daughter, Gloria. In Guadalajara, was it? On that corner in her dream there was a children's clothing shop like something out of the nineteenth century with elegant items that caught her attention. Ana María picked out the loveliest pieces for her granddaughter. In the dream, she was certain that she would see the little girl as soon as she returned from her trip and could give her the dresses made of tulle, organza, lace, bone-colored silk, white linen, silver and gold embroidery, tiny flowers embroidered in ochre silk thread. The dresses seemed like they belonged in a museum, like they were made for aristocrats. In her dream, as she selected clothing for her granddaughter, who she knew was at home, Ana María wondered what would happen if she were to start her own line of children's clothing. For the first time in the seven months her granddaughter had been missing, Ana María had no doubt that she was on the radar, that she was home with her daughter and son-in-law, so she added a few ribbons and bows to her purchase. She was absolutely certain she would soon be able to put this finery on little Gloria, whom she was desperate to see, as if the child's return would bring her peace of mind not only about her granddaughter but also about her darling twins.

Ana María awoke a bit earlier than usual, while it was still dark out, and touched the little satchel of salt La Jefa had given her, disoriented for a moment and unsure whether her granddaughter was home with her daughter and son-in-law or not. The first thing she did after sunrise was call her daughter to see if there had been any news the night before, but Gloria just burst into tears on the other end of the line. Seven months had gone by, and they knew nothing about the whereabouts of Ana María's granddaughter, who was almost three years old by then. And yet she had a feeling, or rather, she was certain that something was about to happen and had no doubt that it would be good news. Her granddaughter was about to appear. May the wheel of fortune spin the world as it sometimes does, bringing us to our best destiny even when we're standing still.

13.

IN EARLY SEPTEMBER OF THE YEAR 1946, MR. GUSTAVO Miranda received a call from the reporter José Córdova asking him to meet at the office of Captain Rubén Darío Hernández the next morning. When Mr. Miranda arrived, Hernández could be seen through the glass panel in the door to his office talking with the reporter. Mr. Miranda entered and closed the door behind him. Hernández called in Ignacio Rodríguez Guardiola. Rumors began to fly around Special Operations that they had found the girl. A few minutes later, the four men took their leave of one another; Córdova accompanied Mr. Miranda on his way out, but they were stopped in the entrance by a journalist who was covering the wave of kidnappings for a small newspaper. She asked them if the girl had been found. José Córdova pulled her aside and, as Mr. Miranda kept walking, told her that they couldn't reveal any details at the moment, said something about a code of ethics and that he hoped she would understand, and then requested her discretion. But the reporter approached Octavio, who was tying one of his rigorously polished boots, and asked if he had any information about the girl. The whole time Octavio was telling her what he knew, she never took her eyes off his cleft lip.

The next morning, reporters crowded around the door to

Special Operations, waiting for Captain Rubén Darío Hernández to arrive. One of the other officers called him at home to say he had an audience waiting to hear him recite the poetry he knew by heart. That same morning, several radio announcers speculated about the girl's possible rescue, and a few even ventured guesses about how she had been found. Stirred again, the waters of public opinion were murky. That afternoon saw the publication of the first column that talked about how important it was that the Mexico City police force handle such a difficult case with care and precision. According to the columnist, it was a national concern because the state should be able to keep children safe; otherwise, it was a sign that Miguel Alemán's government was handing over its power to criminal elements from the very start.

The next morning, Captain Rubén Darío Hernández was mentioned several times in the newspaper and had reporters waiting for him at the entrance to Special Operations, where he did not appear for a second day. The rumors multiplied. By the afternoon, more reporters had gathered outside Special Operations waiting for an official announcement, but no one inside was authorized to comment on the Gloria Miranda Felipe case.

On Saturday, September 7, 1946, at 11:11 in the morning, the reporter José Córdova arrived at the offices of Special Operations with little Gloria Miranda Felipe in his arms. A few steps behind them was Captain Rubén Darío, with stains on his shirt that could have been either carrot juice or birria, who knows, and two police officers with an individual in custody; the press assumed it was the kidnapper but—again, who knows—that still wasn't clear. Within a few minutes, Mrs. Gloria Felipe and Mr. Gustavo Miranda ran in, ignoring the questions that the reporters, predominantly men, threw into the air. Ana María Felipe entered in a rush, leaving a trail of some light, floral perfume behind her. The girl had been rescued a mere hour and a half earlier, and news-rooms were already preparing headlines and layouts as they waited for the whole story. What happened? Who did it? How? Why? Where had the girl been all this time?

PART TWO

In this section, given the limitations of my role as a third-person narrator, I will transcribe the following statements in first person, just as I did when recounting Ana María's visit to La Jefa, who was, in the end, right about the girl being found before six moons had passed. Anyway, this is what Captain Rubén Darío Hernández said to the press:

ESTEEMED MEMBERS OF THE PRESS, THANK YOU FOR joining us here today. We realize that this case has garnered national attention and are very pleased to announce that Gloria Miranda Felipe, two years and eight months of age, was found alive after seven months and three weeks and returned to her family. The child presents no physical or psychological injuries. On the twenty-second of January of this year, in the context of the wave of kidnappings that has plagued our nation of late, we added this little girl to our list of missing children. Of the twenty-seven cases opened by Special Operations, we have rescued eighteen minors, including Gloria Miranda Felipe. Let me take this opportunity to reiterate that we are committed to finding each and every one of the missing children. As you are aware, esteemed members of the press, from the outset a financial reward was offered for any clues that might lead to the location of Gloria Miranda Felipe. At this time, I would like to publicly recognize the outstanding work of José Córdova, the reporter who played a key role in the child's rescue. He was steadfast in his collaboration with Special Operations, determined to rebuild our society in the face of these terrible attacks on the homes and families that are the heart of our beloved Mexico. Esteemed members of the press, in January of the present

131

year I sent police officers to different neighborhoods of our great city in order to gather information regarding the abduction of minors. These officers, on my orders, disguised themselves as clowns, bakers, bums, shoeshines, newspaper and lottery ticket vendors, and security guards at nursery schools. I even sent a few in animal costumes to a children's hospital, three daycare centers, and seven schools in this important service to the nation. Likewise on my orders, these officers frequented local bars and pulquerías, as I myself also did, in search of the kidnappers. My case files contain reports from public gardens, parks, fairs, circuses, moving picture houses, and theaters. It was thanks to these reports that we were able to locate the eighteen minors of whom I speak. I would also like to call your attention, esteemed members of the press, to the great feat our society has achieved, because a home that recovers its children is the home we call Mexico today. Thank you for your applause, my friend. Please allow me to commend the extraordinary efforts of Officer Ignacio Rodríguez Guardiola, badge number 576, who, disguised as a mail carrier, discovered the residence where Gloria Miranda Felipe was being held in privation of her liberty. Large windows allowed a clear line of sight into a ground-floor apartment at 31 Calle Violeta in Colonia Guerrero, within which a little girl bearing a suspicious resemblance to Gloria Miranda Felipe gazed out at the street while two adults played cards in one of the rooms behind her. Her resemblance to the girl for whom this department of Special Operations had been searching since January twenty-second of this year struck the officer as strange, but stranger still was the child's behavior, insofar as she was not playing outside like other children. Consequently, Officer Rodríguez Guardiola returned to the residence several times over the course of the following week, delivering counterfeit letters that I myself composed right here in this building, and he took the liberty of asking why the minor never played with other children. During this same period, Special Operations honed the minutiae and details of the girl's rescue. And so it was that Special Operations, with the collaboration of the police and benefitting from the investigation and commitment of the reporter José Córdova, formulated a plan in the very department where you favor us with your presence today, esteemed members of the press. At first, it appeared that the name of the minor at that address did not match our case file. It was the neighbors who informed this department of Special Operations that the missing girl was the very same one watching the other children play through the window. That was when we went to the civil registry and confirmed we were indeed dealing with none other than Gloria Miranda Felipe. As the ranking officer in this case of tremendous national importance, I wish I could provide further details, but my department still needs to conduct a few final interrogations. Let me then reiterate the most important point on this day, September the seventh of the present year, for all my compatriots: Gloria Miranda Felipe was rescued by the police force of this Mexico we are rebuilding toward a prosperous tomorrow. Thank you for your applause, my friend. Until the next time I address you regarding this issue of national importance, esteemed members of the press, I have no more to say for the moment but to thank you for the interest you have shown in this case, which is a shining example of the hard work and dedication of the police force in dealing with the delicate and above all serious matter of crimes against minors. Our great city is safe in the hands of the police and the department of Special Operations and, together with the president of the republic, Miguel Alemán Valdés, we assert that our great city is greater today and safer for our children, who are the future of this sweet land. I leave you with the words of our national poet, Ramón López Velarde:

Sweet land, I love you not as myth
but for the communion of your truth,
as I love the girl who peers through the rails
in a blouse buttoned to her ears
and a skirt to her ankle of fine percale.

Thank you, friends and colleagues on the police force, for your applause and whistles. Now to wrap up our interrogations, which are being carried out in collaboration with all those involved in the case. As soon as we prepare the reports, esteemed members of the press, you'll be called back to this very place, and I'll share our findings.

This is what Josefina López, building administrator at La Mascota on Calle Bucareli in Colonia Juárez—they're called municipalities now, rather than colonies, but let's not get hung up on that—said to Officer Ignacio Rodríguez Guardiola and the typist Guadalupe Orellano:

WHAT DO I KNOW, YOUNG MAN, ALL I KNOW IS HOW my mother, may she rest in peace, always said to me, Josefina, you're a real nosy Nellie but don't get mixed up in other people's business. What you're asking me, go ask the Poet or that reporter, they were there. If you want to ask me something, ask me about the gossip, young man, I know it all. It's not for nothing they call me the Goddess of Gab, in all modesty, young man. In the market, I mean. Just like you do your job in an office, the juiciest gossip gets served up piping hot for a good price in the market, young man. It's one thing to be the Queen but a whole other thing to be the Goddess, and that's me, in the flesh. If I dished all the dish I know, you'd have a book right there, young man, fatter than the Bible and all of it juicy. So, like I said, I don't know nothing about what you're asking, you could go ask some rocks and they'd know more than me about all that, but you've got the newspapers for reading about what happened. Everyone in Mexico knows about what happened to the Miranda Felipe family, I mean, it was a huge deal, their little girl got kidnapped. I don't think you really get it, young man. Seven months she was kidnapped, seven long months, can't you see that's a lifetime for a mother? But what do you know about all that, young as you are, young man. Here I am,

135

on the other side of my flashes, a grandmother to two rug rats from my son, but I'd wager you've never needed to scrape your heart off the floor. Never been flattened like a doormat. What could you know about life? You haven't lived. I mean, you haven't even offered me a tequila, and here I am trotting out the boleros with nothing but water to wet my whistle. Am I right? I'm saying I don't know donkey about numbers, so don't ask me, young man, if you want numbers go play the lottery, there's lots of numbers there. Me, you should ask about who picked a fight with who, who left who, who was seen with who. I mean, it's my job to notice things, they pay me to watch the building and the Good Lord blessed me with the pleasure of seeing everything else. No, listen, there was none of that, those two were in God's hands, Mr. and Mrs. Miranda Felipe were like churchyard doves. Good people, and their five children are good people, too. Hardworking. The oldest boy even mops and dusts! I've seen him do it with my own eyes. Just like you see me right in front of you, I've seen him cook and everything, and when they took little Gloria he even helped Consuelo watch his brothers. I saw him helping her and said to myself, someone give me half a dozen like that one. My own son, don't get me started. It's a miracle if that boy ever made his own bed. She's a good woman, that Consuelo, not like me. I don't take orders. If someone's going to give me an order, it had better be an order of tacos. Am I right, young man? A good woman, though. I bet that one could turn an atheist into a priest with her goodness. Now, Mrs. Ana María has a ton of cash. A whole ton. They say she's one of the richest women around. Real distinguished. She has heaps of money and always goes around in a hat and gloves, silk stockings, and high heels clackity-clacking here and there. A real Midas touch, she has, buying up this house here, that business there . . . They say she buys houses like most people buy limes. By the dozen, young man. That building where she has her wedding gown shop and the beauty parlor are hers . . . She rents her other shops but they say she also makes money on other properties she owns. Who knows what people do with that much dough, am I right? She makes clothes and puts people's hair up in buns. The most expensive buns in Mexico, that's for sure. Maybe a few sequins here, a few beads there, a little flounce or some lace, maybe a little bird there in your bun, or better yet, let's stick a whole molcajete in there with a bird nesting inside. One time, I told her. I said, Ma'am, not even the night sky with all its stars is as beautiful as the dress you have on, because it did look like the night sky, and the sequins on it were placed even better than the stars in the sky, because she makes dresses even better than God makes the night, sometimes he doesn't add any stars at all because who knows, maybe he's stingy, but before every big party women line up to order their dresses from Mrs. Ana María, and each one costs a month's rent. They say that even before her granddaughter was found, she had already made the clothes she's wearing in that picture. I say who wants to dress their brats in fine clothing if they're just going to pee all over it, am I right, Lupe? In that photograph they took of little Gloria, the one they took for the afternoon papers, she's wearing a dress Mrs. Ana María made for her. That's the one. But they say it was already made before she was found. They say Ana María had already made the dress before the girl was brought back. They say she knew her granddaughter was going to be rescued on such-and-such date at such-and-such time because she went to see a bruja who said, Your granddaughter will be found on such-and-such date at such-and-such time, and heaven forbid she appear in the newspaper in a dress she outgrew a year earlier, oh no, heaven forbid, and so she made the child a fine little frock, am I right? They say she even told the reporters to hold their horses because she'd forgotten the girl's ribbon, and Miss Beatriz ran off to get the ribbon so Mrs. Ana María could put in on the girl for the photo and she could look well cared for when she appeared in the newspapers in her fine little dress. If only, am I right, Lupe? If only our biggest problem in life was putting on the right clothes. Miss Beatriz? She helped the Miranda Felipe family with their calls and their paperwork a few times, yes. I saw her come and go with these here eyes, wearing this here dress. She's Mrs. Ana María's right-hand man. Or is it right-hand lady? They say Mrs. Ana María went to see a bruja. They also say she's some kinda bruja, herself. That she reads her clients' numbers and their palms. What do I know, young man, I can't even read a book. Palms, imagine. Rich people always want to have everything read, their cups of tea, even the hairs on their soap, am I right? But in the market they say Mrs. Ana María reads the numbers and the palms of her clients. They say she tells the ladies, That's a boy in your belly or a girl in your belly, or that's just tacos in your belly, and she's always right, they say that some of the ladies even made her their baby's godmother and have her to the baptism because she tells them what color clothing to buy their little ones and they even bring their friends and their comadres with them so Mrs. Ana María can tell them boy or girl. They say she uses a medallion, don't ask me. Anyway, they say she went to a bruja, but a real honest-to-goodness bruja, and the bruja-bruja told her how to find her granddaughter and Mrs. Ana María sets to making her granddaughter a dress. Mrs. Ana María's no bruja-bruja, she just knows how to read numbers and hands and how to say whether a belly has a boy in it or a girl or just tacos. I tell you, I don't know from numbers, you go and talk to someone from the lottery, they'll have plenty of numbers to give you. I don't know if all this is useful to you, young man, but I like to spice the soup a bit, if you know what I mean, I like to give it a little kick—and you like it like that, with a kick, am I right? Woo! I just gave myself a craving for some soup, didn't I now. What, you don't want any? Must be losing my touch. Anyway, they say that Mrs. Ana María did something and they found the girl. She's got power, that one. I get embarrassed when I see her, I feel dirty even if my hair's still wet from washing it, because she's so imposing. But can I tell you something? She'd be imposing even in her pajamas. Because that's how she is: always sure of herself, always walking with her back straight, all elegant, and people just get out of her way. Who knows what deals she made, because she only rubs elbows with powerful types and she's all over the newspapers and magazines. They say she talks English and Irish and has her plis and dan-kiu for a cherry on top. She even gets invitations from the president— please join us for dinner, Mrs. Ana María, please join us for breakfast, Mrs. Ana María—and politicians do her favors in exchange for classy dresses for their wives. I'm telling you, she has them all in her pocket. And boy, is she loaded. I've seen her give fancy things to a beggar just because she didn't have change on her at the moment. Loaded. Rolling in dough. I know for a fact that she gives each of her grandchildren a centenary coin every Sunday. Big fat gold coins the size of tortillas she gives them. Rich folks, am I right, young man? That's just how it is. And it shows. You can't hide that kind of rich because gold shines in the light. They say she had a hard life before, real hard, that her husband cheated on her and she said enough's enough and hit the road with her daughter, who was just a little girl back then. She divorced and stayed that way, never took another man. They say she had a whole bunch of suitors, but she didn't care about any of that, all she cared about were her shops. She and I are alike in that, even though I don't have gold coins the size of tortillas to show for it, all I have is the tortillas. And also she's a looker. Between that and all her dough, they say she was the one who made sure everybody, and I mean everybody, heard about her granddaughter's case. There's nothing money can't buy. It buys justice in this country, excuse me for saying so, young man, but it does. Am I right? Prison is for the poor. You've got your Palacio Negro over there, filled to the brim with poor folks. If you ask me, they call it the Black Palace because of skin color. Am I right? I don't see any white people in there. Or do you think you'd ever see someone like Mrs. Ana María in prison? Oh, no, heaven forbid. Sweet baby Jesus. No way. The good thing about these rich people and all their money is they make a big racket because someone stepped on their toe and sometimes that helps everybody. It was like they were filming a movie in the building, like some famous actress lived there, let me tell you, there were so many cameras and reporters. Saw it with my own eyes. I couldn't go out with my apron, I wasn't about to appear on the front page of the newspaper with corn flour all over my apron, was I, young man? I may be poor, but I'm twice as vain. Always neat and tidy. Being humble isn't the same thing as being good, I don't want anyone calling me humble when what they mean is poor, because I've got vanity and dignity by the boatload and I spread them around like the rich spread their money. If I'm here talking with you, just imagine how things were, especially with those so-called kidnappers who only wanted Mrs. Ana María's money. They even sent Mrs. Gloria a shoe just like the one her little girl was wearing that day. Poor thing, with my own eyes I saw her praying over that little shoe. The Poet said it was the little girl's case that got the other ones moving, that there was no more kicking the ball down the road because the pots were boiling over. A real pressure cooker. Plus, they needed to make a good impression on the new president. Everyone makes a fuss over dough, but what about us poor folks, we don't get so much as a "thank you," am I right? It's poor folks doing our work down here in the sewers, dark-skinned folks like me and you, what am I telling you for, I saw you out there singing for your soup dressed up like a mailman. Lucky thing you weren't disguised as a clown, just imagine catching the crook with his finger in the pie and you on the front page with a red nose on, dressed like a clown and you getting famous like that in the papers with your big floppy shoes. I won't lie to you, I was real happy when they found little Gloria, I'd prayed a hundred times to the patron saint of families, asking Saint Anthony of Padua for a miracle, because it's one thing, you know, for the Poet to chase Mrs. Ana María's dough, and this is a whole other thing, if you don't mind my saying so. And him acting all righteous for finding the little girl when it was really the cash he was after. I wasn't born yesterday, you can't hook me with just any old bait, that's why they call me the Goddess of Gab. So you go ahead and ask me your questions, Mr. Pencils, Mr. Write-this-down, Mr. Type-this-up-Lupe, put what the lady says in your machine, Lupe, but Mrs. Ana María buys everything with her dough, or are you going to try and tell me she didn't buy her granddaughter's rescue? What can I say? Cops love to be greased and everybody knows it. You can write that down, Lupe. And the Poet has a wife and kid just like the reporter, that's the one, Córdova, he's not so hard on the eyes, am I right, Lupe? He's married, too, to a woman named Brenda, and they've got two little ones. I saw the Poet and the reporter all the time here in the building. One time I even made them coffee and asked all about their missus. Yes, Brenda. They give girls who No-Speek-Inglich such strange names here in Mexico, God knows why. Anyway, the reporter and his wife Brenda-in-Inglich have two daughters, and the Poet has one son. You should have seen how they got on with Mrs.

Ana María and how they made their deals with her. You might
not want to hear this, young man, but I have to say it: Mrs. Ana
María is more the boss than the bosses are. They say that when she
went to see the bruja who gives politicians animal blood to drink
like it was birria—I'm getting hungry, aren't you, Lupe?—the
bruja told her where the girl was and she told the Poet and the
reporter. And they told you, Go here dressed like a mailman to
keep up appearances, but they already knew, they needed a story
to tell and off you went to put your face on the evening papers. I'm
a Catholic, Roman Apostolic, may God keep me, and all this
business about witches seems full of shadow. All cold and stinky,
like fish are full of shadow. The thing is, young man, I can't eat a
bite of fish, it's terrible for me, like the devil himself, it is. And the
coast, which is where I'm from, well that's like hell itself, with so
many fish. Anyway, someone told you to go to Colonia Guerrero
to what's-its-name street and to do whatever there disguised as a
mailman. Mrs. Ana María went to rub mule's blood on herself
and dance like a worm on the griddle so the shadows would tell
her where to find her granddaughter, and that's why you got sent
where you got sent. You and I both know that in this country
money talks, and nobody walks. And that's never good for people
who look like us: it's good for people who are white, skinny, attractive. I should know, with my dark skin and my waistline like
an icebox. The world is for people like Mrs. Ana María—I mean,
how does she look so good at sixty and always well fed, well
dressed, well perfumed? Am I right? I'll bet she sleeps with her
heels on and her lips painted red and wakes up saying, Goodness,
what a looker I am, where's my coffee? And two servants in servants' uniforms—heaven forbid someone confuses them for someone with money, heaven forbid they use the stairs reserved for rich
folks, sweet baby Jesus, no—bring her coffee and an egg on a silver

dish, and if she woke up with a craving, a third servant brings her slices of papaya. If only, Lupe. Am I right? Imagine people bringing you food, when here we are having to chase it down day in and day out, nobody handing us anything on a silver platter. If only life were like Mrs. Ana María's life, just worrying about clothing and hairstyles. Am I right? I've worked in this building longer than you've been on this planet, young man. They say the devil knows more because he's old than because he's the devil, but he'd know even more if he liked gossip as much as I do. He doesn't mess around, the devil, he's more serious than a toothache, just look at how he scares the daylights out of everyone, and that's without this talent I have by the boatload. You see why I love my job so much, young man? I learn a lot about people's lives. I'm the kind of woman who will follow someone down the street because they're spilling some interesting beans. I don't like to be kept in suspense. I'm the one who gets the dirt on what the bastard did to the girl who's pouring out her heart to the other girl. Now just imagine, the building where I work is right in the eye of the hurricane. Mrs. Gloria just wasted away after her little girl was taken, and I and everybody else thought the worst at one point, imagine what she must have thought, God have mercy I say, as a mother and a grandmother. They said she'd been kidnapped, they even said she'd been murdered because the ransom hadn't been paid, they said it was her fault because she put too many fake bills in with the real. She had a hard time, a real hard time. And then the next day her neighbor in the next apartment over hightailed it out of there. A gringa, a blue-eyed Catrina with her three kids saying, Gud-by my friends, look sharp out there. But you wouldn't understand, young man, not even when you have children of your own because no one knows a mother's suffering except other mothers, and it's only because I have a little one who has his own little one that I can put myself in poor Mrs. Gloria's shoes and tell you the hell she went through. There's nothing worse that can happen to a mother. That's why I offered to help her. She took some medicine that washed her eyes out, left them like lukewarm eggs. I picked up her medicine for her a few times from the pharmacy. Once I even took one and spent the whole day smiling, with a wicked urge to dance. She lost a lot of weight. I know she stopped eating because I watched her get thinner and thinner, like a bar of soap she wasted away. Used to be that she'd come and go with shopping bags full of food for her children, but I tell you what, now it's the oldest son, Gustavo like his father, who took over with Consuelo. The youngest, Carlos, he's the one closest to the little girl. And Mr. Gustavo, back and forth between the telephone company, his house, and the police station. We all want one like him. I mean, I don't, not anymore, but you should take note, Lupe, that one's a good father and a good husband, I've seen it with my own eyes, I've seen it while wearing this here dress. Mrs. Ana María between her trips, her society events, and the ransom for those so-called kidnappers. I don't know how much, if it's numbers you want, young man, you're better off asking somewhere else. Go ask the lottery, they have plenty of numbers. What I'd like to know, Mr. Policeman, is who was that man who arrived with Mrs. Ana María, because I never saw him before. Never. I knew right away that they hadn't done anything to the little girl. I even heard that she called the people who took her "grandma" and "grandpa." Mrs. Ana María doesn't let her own grandchildren call her "grandma," that's how vain she is. It's always Ana María this and Ana María that. But the little girl did call her kidnapper "grandma." It's a lucky thing they treated her like a grandchild and didn't touch a hair on her head, that really is a thing for thanking God. That's what I'm saying. Yes, that's what I said. No woman should ever have to go through the pain Mrs. Gloria and Mr. Gustavo went through, I know because I saw how they suffered. What I'm saying is that it's not right how things get resolved by throwing money around. I'm saying that the problem is this country, where things get resolved that way, am I right? The kidnappers are headed to the Black Palace. And rightly so, I'm not saying they don't deserve it. The law exists for a reason, young man. That's why we're here chewing the fat, am I right? I'm just saying that there's something wrong with this country when kidnapped children get rescued by throwing heaps of money around. That what's wrong in this country is that justice can be bought. And I think the problem starts with God our Father, because he only took seven days to make this world and clearly that wasn't enough time to do a good job of it, just look at the mess he left us. He should have taken at least two weeks to make the world, am I right? Forget seven days, you give me seven minutes, a mop, and a bucket, and you'll see how nice I leave this office, even the entryway where all those reporters danced the jarabe tapatío with all their questions. Just imagine. That's what they get for leaving the world to God Almighty instead of to the Goddess of Gab, because that would have been a whole other story. A more entertaining one, at least. Or are you saying you like your coffee black? Everything's better with a little sugar, am I right?

This is what Hortensia García García, the twelve-year-old girl implicated in the kidnapping of Gloria Miranda Felipe, said to reporter José Córdova:

YES. YES, IT WAS ME, SIR. IT WAS ME, SIR. I TOOK THE girl. Got paid well for it, too. I hadn't ever been able to give my mother so much money before. It was a good opportunity. The opportunity, sir. That kind of money doesn't turn up every day, sir. Yes, my brother and I take care of her. He's fourteen years old already, and I'll turn thirteen at the end of the month. Yes, sir. She's forty-six. Wait, forty-seven. Yes, sir. In a wheelchair. Has been for a few years already. Six, sir. Yes. Just water, please, sir. I'm not hungry. Pardon? I do like pastries, sir, but I'm not hungry. Anyway, my mom's in a wheelchair, she was run over by a car. Here and here. They had to amputate her leg. Yes, she met the lady there. They're friends from work. My mom's a nurse. Was a nurse. I mean, she's still a nurse, but she can't work anymore. She knows how to cure us when we get sick, but my brother and I are the ones who take care of her. I don't know who my father is. My mom says he was a doctor, but my brother and I don't know him. My mom says he died, but my brother says he saw him one day with another family in La Alameda, with kids who were older than us. My brother says that those other kids look just like us, but that our father ignored him when he shouted "Papá." Scram, kid, he said, like my brother was a street dog begging for scraps. We don't

147

know anyone from my father's family, we don't even know their names. No, sir. My mom and my grandpa, may he rest in peace, but then my brother and I had to start taking care of my mom. No, sir, she never married. My grandpa was like a father to me. Now the three of us live alone. My brother works, he does deliveries and takes whatever odd jobs he can. Same as me. We had to stop going to school. I only got to grade school. My brother, too. Grade school, sir. What do we need more schooling for if what we need is food on the table? That's why we help out. Pardon? Yes, she has a pension, but it's not enough, sir. I bathe my mother and make our food. My brother wakes her up and puts her to bed and gives her all her medicine. Yes, sir. She and the lady are friends. That's how I know her. One day she came looking for me and invited me out for a snack. I don't know, sir, I didn't check the name. Churros and coffee. Sometimes a sandwich. No, that's what I like. I like churros and cappuccinos with lots of milk. The lady came to pick me up and took me to have a snack. She paid for everything and even let me order some churros to bring back for my mom and my brother, which lasted us until breakfast the next day. That was when she asked me to help her find families with lots of kids because they needed one for adoption. That's what she said, sir. No, I didn't know, sir. She told me how much she would pay me. It was a whole lot, sir. Two hundred pesos, sir. I hadn't ever brought so much money home, sir. I said yes and after mom's bath I went out looking in parks where I usually see kids playing. I spent my mornings there, sir. Yes, that's how it was. I'm telling you the truth, sir. I went to different parks and saw families with lots of kids. One after another. Wealthy families, sir. Yes. First I saw a family in Condesa with a lot of kids, the lady told me the family should have lots of kids and that I should pay close attention to the youngest. I will, I said. That's right, sir, I did what she asked for two hundred pesos. After giving my mom a bath I would go to the park in Colonia Condesa to watch the kids. There was one family with eight children and the mother of the eight children was pregnant. They were going to be nine. I told the lady that in the place she took me for snacks. Pardon? Yes, sir. I told her that it was a family with eight children and that the mother of the eight children was pregnant. But there was something weird. I had never seen anyone wear little hats like the ones they wore. Yes, sir, like that. Little round black things, flat on their heads like mats. Yes. I don't know, I guess I thought it was strange, sir. No, sir, I didn't know. And the boys were dressed like grownups, but in miniature, all of them in black pants and white shirts, all the same and with white strings sticking out. I don't know. I don't think so. I never saw it before. And the mother of those eight kids was pregnant and she dressed like she was from another place and wore a wig. I could tell, sir. The next time the lady bought me a snack, I told her about the eight kids, but she said I should maybe look somewhere else. I don't know why. But that's what I did, sir. I went to another park. I walked all the way to Colonia Juárez because that's where rich people live. Lots of them have five kids, or even more. I saw the mother in the park with the girl and her other kids and I played with them and the woman left us playing. I only waved hello, sir. I wasn't going to say anything to her, sir. But then we ended up playing there. And later, at the snack shop, I told the lady that maybe I found the family. She said she wanted to see them first. Yes, sir, I told her where to find them. Pardon? Yes. Then later she came over to my house and said the girl was cute and rosy-cheeked. Yes, sir. Rosy-cheeked. Those were her exact words. And she said it was the little girl she wanted. I would go to the park in the mornings after I gave mom her bath. Yes, I do like kids. I would love to work in a daycare one day, but I don't have enough school. My dream is to be a grade-school teacher, sir, but I have to take care of my mom and put food on the table for her and my brother. I like kids and I like to study, sir, but I can't. We weren't made for going to school. But I enjoyed playing with the kids and became friends with the girl. That park is where the kids who live in all those houses and buildings go to play, sir. When they leave the courtyard of their buildings, that's where they go. The lady offered me four hundred pesos to gain the family's trust, so that's what I did, sir. We ate meat at home. No, sir, we don't usually get to eat meat. We bought fresh milk and eggs, and by the grace of God there was enough food. We made coffee with lots of milk for my mom and listened to the radio together at night. A radio drama. My brother and I took her to the store and I bought her a dress she wanted, and I bought my brother pants and a shirt and black leather shoes. And I bought myself something, too, sir. I had always wanted a white dress because I never got to take catechism or have my first communion. I bought myself a white dress to wear on Sundays. Yes, sir, six hundred pesos in total so far. One day in the snack shop the lady told me, Do it tomorrow. The third payment would be two thousand five hundred pesos. Yes, sir, I'd already spent the first two, even though my mother had saved a little bit in a jar so we could buy food. Yes, sir. Do it tomorrow, she said, and she told me how. She gave me some chalk and told me to play hopscotch with the girl during her usual play-time. She also gave me some pills, sir. I already knew that the woman returned home in the morning after dropping off her other kids at school, so I knew what time I would find the girl there to play with. I put on a gray dress. No, sir, I only wear the white one on Sundays, and that was a Tuesday. Yes, sir, she gave me pills and told me to play with the little girl until her mother left and then to give her a pill so she'd go to sleep and then bring her in a taxi to where the lady was waiting. And that's what I did. It was easy, sir. Pardon? Yes, it happened just like I said. Yes, easy. Pills and chalk for hopscotch. Really, sir, a piece of cake. The mother and the woman who works in the building weren't there, and I just told the taxi driver that the girl was my little sister. Yes, sir, I was able to carry her. She wasn't heavy at all. I lift my mom, sir, I bathe her and change her clothes and wash them. I take her to the bathroom and help her do her business. Yes, sir. She has a pension from when she was a nurse, but it's not enough. And right around then, she was starting to really need an operation on her hip. Yes, sir, right around then.

We needed money, sir. There was no other way. My mom can't walk, but the operation would help with her pain. Yes, sir. We were going to use the money for the doctor. A week after, with that money. Yes, sir. No. I never saw her again. No, sir, I didn't ask. She was a nice lady. Adoption is good. Yes, I do think so, sir. Helping my mom is good. She gave me the money and I never saw her again, sir. Yes, I did hear something on the radio. Yes. Yes, I did figure out it was the girl I took. That was when the lady came looking for me at night. You're right, I did see her again. My brother was feeding mom a little snack and I was fixing one of her skirts when the lady knocked on our door. Yes, she told me right outside my door. She told me she would pay me another two thousand five hundred pesos if I didn't say a word, sir. Not me or my mom or my brother. And so we didn't say a word, sir. But I hadn't told my mom or my brother how I'd gotten the money. I just told them I had a job helping someone. No, sir. If you need money and you help someone, it's a favor and a job. The whole thing only took fifteen minutes, sir. It was easy. No, sir. It's different. I'm talking with you now because I kept my promise. I didn't say anything because the lady paid me not to say anything, sir. We still have a little bit of that money left. After mom's operation and after buying food. You offered me money so that what I'm saying to you know can be printed in your newspaper, sir. I'm doing you a favor, too, sir. You need to put food on the table, too, sir. And you're paying me, too. It was easy, sir. Yes, I would do it again. I don't regret it, sir. I didn't do anything wrong. I won't go to jail, sir, because I didn't do anything wrong, and also because I'm twelve. Almost thirteen. I helped the lady and I helped my family, sir, just like I'm helping you make a living with my story.

This is what Nuria Valencia said to Captain Rubén Darío Hernández:

THERE'S NO GREATER FORCE IN THE WORLD THAN desire. There's nothing more dangerous than a mother. You don't understand me, you could never understand. I can't have children, but that's also a way of being a mother, because my desire is so strong. I went to different doctors and all of them told me I would never be a mother. You're barren, they said. They all said I'm barren. You're young but barren, they said, and I felt old. They told me I would never be a mother. I tried to adopt a child at the orphanage, but I realized that their forms weren't going to let me be a mother, either. Do you have any idea how complicated it is to adopt a child? No, you don't understand. They gave me the runaround. Around and around and then nothing. Going to see children and babies at the orphanage, knowing I'll never be able to bring one home. A rainbow the color of ash. They loaned us a little boy named Efraín. Yes. We treated a disease he had in his eyes. My boss helped us get him into the Children's Hospital. Yes, thanks to him. Yes, that's his name. No one would adopt him, everyone was frightened away by the disease he had in his eyes. I heard he got adopted and that his new family took him to live in Guadalajara. Little Efraín sent us a letter last month. He remembered us. He ate churros in Guadalajara and he thought of us. My

153

boss is a good man. Why that girl? I liked the look of her and knew that Mrs. Felipe had a few children, what difference would one less make to her? She had five children already, what difference would it make to her if she had one less? Yes, Officer, that's what I thought. What would she care? Yes. And besides, she could always make another, or even two or three, but I couldn't. This is why I understand the sea. Because the sea moves whatever it needs to in order to get where it wants to go. I chose the youngest so she'd barely be able to speak or remember her home. Forty years in prison is nothing compared to not being a mother. I understand the sea. No, that doesn't matter. Look at me. It doesn't matter. You don't understand the sea. Look at me: some crimes are worth the punishment. Nothing glows brighter in the night than a star, and an unfulfilled desire is the darkest night of all. My crime is worth it for the star it brought me. No, it wasn't like that. I swear. Those laws were not written by women. I don't care. What do you want me to say? I don't care. And here we are. My husband's out there, and my parents, and my mother-in-law, too. Yes, her name is Agustina, we named our daughter after her. It doesn't matter. Nothing they can do to me matters, forty years in prison is nothing for the chance to care for a daughter. That's why I understand the sea at night. Don't throw my husband or my parents or my mother-in-law in jail. No. No, I tell you. No. They had nothing to do with it. I acted alone, Officer. As alone as the moon in the night sky. I did the whole thing by myself. They didn't do anything. I'm telling you straight out, but no matter how clearly I say it, you still don't understand. Crystal clear like fresh water I told you about my problem, about how they told me I was barren. My problem isn't you, Officer, my problem is the law because the same rules that wouldn't allow me to adopt are sending me to prison for forty years. My problem isn't going to jail. No. How do all of you define the end? Death? Prison? Those things aren't the end, Officer. Those things don't matter. They melt away like ice and what's left is water, that's how I felt after taking care of that little girl. You're not understanding me, officer. How could you understand me? My problem isn't you, it's that I can't be a mother. They told me I'm young but barren, and what good to me is a life of flowerless seeds? You know what I mean. Just because you're over there and I'm over here doesn't give you the right to speak to me like that. I'm talking to you clear as water. Water is clear, it's people like you who stir it up until you can't see. I already told you I don't care. Yes of course I saw the newspapers, we have them delivered every day where I work. I read that she couldn't drink milk and she didn't drink a drop of milk the whole time she was with me. It doesn't matter. I mean, I didn't do it because of that. I did it because I had no other choice. But the law doesn't understand that, and you could never understand that, because you're not a woman. Those laws weren't written by women. I had no other choice. None. How many times do you want me to say it? No, I'm not sick, Officer. I'm not. I didn't kill anyone. I told you so many times already. No, Martín had no idea how I did it. We never talked about it. If he figured out what was going on, he never said anything to me. If you're married, then you know that couples don't always say everything out loud to each other, but they always know. It wasn't as urgent for him. Leave him alone. Martín is a good person, a good man. He liked being the girl's father. You don't deserve to know that my husband is an honorable man, but I'm telling you anyway because I want you to know that there are men in the world with honor and good in their souls, not like you. I hope he takes good care of my mother-in-law and my parents, who don't deserve this sorrow. I already told you, no. No one knew but me and God. I was alone like the moon in the night. They had

.no reason to know. Why should they? That doesn't matter. I've told you, no. That's not it. We treated that little girl like the daughter she was to us. A star. Whatever you want to call it. She received that love, whatever name you want to put on it. She was my daughter, and my husband's. She was ours. The fact that I didn't give birth to her doesn't mean that I didn't treat her like my daughter. You don't understand. How could you possibly understand? No, I don't want any peanuts. No, Officer, we never once mistreated the girl. To the contrary, we gave her all the love and care every daughter deserves. Yes, she did learn to call us Mami and Papi, just like we called her our little girl. Agustina, after my mother-in-law. Agustina Fernández Valencia, yes, my night star. That little girl is my star and I'm sure she is for Martín, too. Yes, she called my parents Grandma and Grandpa. No, she called Martín's mother Tina. Yes, Tina. Agustina Mendía. No. No, not at all. She's seventy, I think. Or seventy-one? She lives in Xochimilco. My parents moved in with us. Gonzalo Valencia and Carmela Pérez de Valencia. He's fifty-seven and owns a hardware store. She's a housewife. Yes, fifty-three. From Morelos. Cuernavaca. That's where I grew up, out in the countryside, before coming to the capital. With us. They came after the girl arrived. I asked them to. He works at his hardware store and she's a housewife. That doesn't matter. She lives off her pension. Yes, she worked. Martín's mother lives off her pension, yes. That doesn't matter. I'm not going to answer that because it's none of your business whether my mother-in-law was ever with other men. She's family and I won't say another word. It doesn't matter. No. Yes, I've worked with him for years. Twelve years, at the hospital. Mexico General. No, he didn't know anything. I don't think. Or maybe he heard about it in the newspaper. No, he didn't do anything. No, he wasn't involved. I told you already that he's an important man. Yes, they named a wing of the hospital after him. My boss is a generous man and he cured the disease Efraín had in his eyes so he could be adopted. Yes, Efraín was adopted, I already told you that. No, that's what I'm telling you. No. Not that, either. Yes, he was aware we had adopted a little girl. Yes, he asked me how she was. Just like everyone close to me did. Nothing, just that we'd adopted a little girl. I'm telling you, I acted alone. I already told you. Alone like the moon in the night. I told you. Alone like a dry riverbed that not even bugs or dogs will go near. You have no reason to do anything to anyone. Much less to my husband, he had nothing to do with it. My husband trusts me, he's a good man, Officer. I told him it was an adoption, yes. Why would he doubt me? I didn't want to get him in any trouble then, and I don't want to now. He doesn't deserve it. Yes, that's what I said. He didn't do anything but care for that little girl like she was his own. Martín is a wonderful father. That was all he did: love her and take care of her. There's no reason for him to go to jail, Officer. Not him. No, I told you already. The girl? Hortensia García García. Eleven years old. Twelve. You know better than I do, so why don't we just switch places and I can ask you questions. Because frankly . . . Yes. Frankly, you don't understand my position. That's right. No, nothing to do with it. I'm telling you. Well, yes. Listen. Stop asking so many rhetorical questions. I paid Hortensia three thousand one hundred pesos to find the little girl, gain her trust, and bring her to me. She lives in my neighborhood. Close by, yes. She and her brother take care of their mother. Confined to a wheelchair, yes. We met at the hospital. A nurse. She worked with a doctor who was my boss's friend, yes. I offered the girl money with no strings attached and she did everything I said. She went to Colonia Juárez, I think she went to other neighborhoods first, but in the end she chose Juárez and went and played with the children who live in those buildings on the corner of Bucareli, right there in their courtyard with them. Like rivers reach the sea, I knew Hortensia would bring me to my little girl. And she did. She played with them. She's good with children. They played and I could see she enjoyed it, as if she were one of them, even though they'd only just met. Taking care of her mother turned her into an adult and she likes to be around children. One day I said to her, you're working and playing at the same time. And it's true that she worked just like those birds that sing as they search for food. Like that. We saw each other several times. At a little spot called Merendero María. And that's how she did it: by watching. The way a bird joining a flock watches, that's how she joined them, and they welcomed her like a flock. That girl is a bird. I told her, look to the youngest daughter because she's too young for memories or speaking, that's the one I want. And Hortensia said, all right, ma'am. And no, she didn't say a word. Hortensia doesn't talk much, anyway, but money will shut anyone's mouth, Officer. You know this better than anyone. You heard me. You made a pretty sum for yourself by drawing the search out. Or are you trying to tell me that you didn't enjoy taking bribes from one of the richest women in the country? How do I know, you ask? All the higher-ups knew you were being paid and that's why you dragged out the search. My boss spoke with one of your bosses. That's how I know. I see, you don't like what I'm saying. Hortensia and her family were hungry. I knew I didn't need to worry about her. I knew it. I know what it's like. At work? Nothing. Nothing at all. I didn't have to miss work to arrange things with Hortensia. We would meet at Merendero María. Yes, near my house in Colonia Guerrero. I bought her snacks, sandwiches, atole, chocolates, whatever she wanted for her mother and her brother. No, I don't want any peanuts. That was where we arranged things. I went with her when necessary and watched from a distance. Like that, I'd tell her. Not like that. And so on. That was how I explained what to do and that's how we did it. They just played hopscotch. I bought her a box of chalk and paid her. Yes. What was the exact date? You know better than I do. Anyway, she handed the girl over to me asleep. I gave her medicine. Yes. Yes, I used my boss's prescription pad. Yes. Why do you want it? Do you want to frame it or something? No, he never noticed. I knew it was just a sedative and that it wouldn't do the girl any harm. I'm telling you, I didn't want to hurt her. I loved her and wanted to keep her. Adopt her. I wanted my night to always be lit by her star, but you took her from me. Like I said, I bought the medicine with the prescription I wrote. I forged the doctor's signature, Officer. I'm his secretary. Hortensia put the girl to sleep, hid with her, then got into a taxi with her and brought her to the meeting place we'd arranged. The little one was awake by then, and I brought her home with me until she was back to normal. No, she didn't cry much. She adapted. Children adapt the way water covers surfaces, adapting to whatever forms they take. Martín hadn't gotten home from work. What else can I say? Changing her name was easy. Well, then? Why bother asking me? Do whatever you want. That doesn't matter. I know. Listen, I'm not a killer and I'm not crazy. What's crazy are your laws. They weren't written by women, that's why you don't understand me, why none of you understand us. Fine, take me away. What can I say? Your laws are wrong. If you refuse to see that your laws are wrong for us women, then take me away. You don't understand me. How could you understand? Yes. I would do it again. Twice, even if it meant talking to you twice, I would do it all again. The thing I desired most in the world, I had it. For a while. I was a mother for almost a year; I read stories to my little star and sang her to sleep. You can lock me up all you want but let me speak freely. What do you know? The laws are written by men, what do you know about the things a woman longs for, about the strength of desire? What do you know about the strength of the ocean, about the strength of a woman? You're the ones who make the rules, and you don't even understand that you don't understand. You don't want to understand. What difference does it make? It doesn't matter. Take me away, I lived what I needed to. Take me away! I won't be silent for you or for anyone. You can take me to jail but my voice will be free!

PART THREE

We know this is what happened:

AT HALF PAST TWO IN THE AFTERNOON OF TUESDAY, September 10, 1946, Nuria Valencia Pérez was sentenced to twenty years in prison for the kidnapping of a minor. Her husband, Martín Fernández Mendía, was given the most lenient sentence possible of five years for aiding and abetting a criminal act. It usually takes longer to get a verdict—both today and back then— but everything was sped up by the fact that the case had been such a media sensation. In the Ministerio Público, where the sentence was handed down, a respected Catalan lawyer by the name of Lamadrid, who was living in exile in Mexico and had taken the lead on Nuria's case, accompanied his client as she stood, handcuffed, before Gloria Felipe. The whole thing lasted only a few minutes. They didn't exchange a single word. But Gloria Felipe was carrying her daughter in her arms, and the child waved her little hands effusively when she saw Nuria Valencia, stretching toward her as if she were trying to hug her. Gloria Felipe shifted her daughter so the child could no longer look in Nuria's direction, controlling the little girl's position until she began to cry and wail "Mami, Mami" and neither Gloria nor Nuria knew which one of them she meant. Gloria said a few words to the judge, words Nuria also caught, and rushed out as the little girl continued to cry, rejecting her. Reporters had been given access to the proceedings and were taking wave upon wave of photographs of the recently sentenced Nuria Valencia. Only two reporters photographed Martín Fernández, who was in the next room over, handcuffed and sitting in a wooden chair with his eyes glued to the floor.

That same afternoon, Officer Ignacio Rodríguez Guardiola escorted Nuria Valencia and Martín Fernández to Lecumberri Prison on what was then the outskirts of the city. In the environs of the prison there was a store called Forget Me Not with a sign that bore its name written out in large, shadowed letters. When she saw it, Nuria remembered, without a single muscle in her face so much as twitching, how the little girl had wanted to hug her, to be with her. They were received at the maximum-security prison by a woman from the administrative staff whose hair was split down the middle by a part more perfect than life itself. Their next stop was a large office with a picture window, a desk, and two wooden screens resting like lions on either side of the door. Inside, they waited on a leather sofa. Rodríguez Guardiola made a couple of jokes that the woman with the bare face, hair pulled tight, and drooping eyebrows and lashes did not seem to find funny. Martín and Nuria looked around the office. A guard-in-training a full head shorter than the woman, with a baby face, a buzz cut, and a piercing voice arrived and took Martín Fernández Mendía to cell block C, section 1 of the Black Palace. Nuria Valencia Pérez was led by the woman with a perfect part and calculated movements to cell block F, one of the areas designated for female prisoners.

Allow me to provide some background information about this prison. Lecumberri was the main carceral facility in Mexico. It was built of stone and iron like an impenetrable shield in the shape of a star on five hectares of land. For over forty years, a sewage canal ran near the prison; in addition to providing the smell that became synonymous with the place, the moisture gradually blackened its walls. This is, in part, why it came to be known as the Black Palace, but it was known by that name, above all, for the dark stories that lived within its walls.

The star-shaped building was designed as a panopticon, a model popular in the late eighteenth century. At its center was a round yard with a tower from which guards could keep watch in all directions, at all hours. This architecture ended up shaping the conduct of the persons deprived of liberty: they began to behave as if they were being observed at all times. Lecumberri's population was predominantly male, but it was a mixed prison and at the time of Nuria's incarceration there was a total of 286 women and 127 minors inside.

The number of persons deprived of liberty—I use this contemporary term because some words get dusty, they rust with age—far exceeded the prison's capacity, as it had for decades already. Lecumberri had been built with seven hundred cells, but many of those cells were being shared by two or even three people. The wards were long hallways with two levels of cells behind steel doors. Each cell was two and a half meters deep and two meters high with a "sky," as the prisoners called the ceiling, made of galvanized steel, and each contained up to two hanging metal beds outfitted with either a mattress or a simple mat, depending, and a sink and lidless toilet made of glazed cast iron. The administrative offices were in the main building. There were also workshops where men deprived of liberty learned and practiced skills that required physical strength, such as masonry, ironwork, pottery, and carpentry. Each cell block bore a letter over its entryway, and each letter denoted a type of crime or prisoner; for example, the women's units or cell block J, where homosexual individuals were confined—this is why gay men are called "jotos" in Mexico to this day; it should be noted that, despite certain contemporary uses, the term is still considered derogatory, just as it was back then. For the prisoners who lacked the physical strength for the activities mentioned above, including some of the "jotos" (who were also known as "fairies," a fact I'm obligated to share with you as a third-person narrator), there were also workshops for tailors, cobblers, and printers, as well as a haberdashery—hats were an everyday accessory back then. Those individuals who claimed to be "unfit" for such labors were put to work making brooms, baskets, and rope. Women were given space to paint, sew, and embroider. Because they were women. All persons deprived of liberty were supposed to be reintegrated into society with a basic command of one of those skills and the ability to read, add, subtract, multiply, and divide. In that, the genders were equal.

Past the workshops was a long hallway that led to the infirmary; the operating room was a few meters farther, and in the length of hallway that stretched between the two was a long cabinet displaying the skulls of the prisoners who had died within Lecumberri's walls since its solemn inauguration at the dawn of the twentieth century. Among these, Nuria discovered soon after her arrival, were skulls that appeared to have belonged to babies. She wondered how it was possible that babies died, and then, in a movement so swift it was like a bird taking flight after being startled by a noise, she asked herself how it was possible that children, in general, could die. Dozens of accounts from the earliest days of the prison detail crimes that took place within its black stone walls, and some of the skulls were evidence of these. It was called Lecumberri after the man who owned the land on which it was constructed, but by 1946 its nickname, the Black Palace, was synonymous with terror.

The prison was divided into three sections. The first was near the kitchen and the bakery, and it was where the people closest to the date of their release were held. In the middle section were the prisoners employed in the social reintegration workshops, who also needed to take high school equivalency classes in the afternoons. In the final section, located at the tip of the star, which is to say at the anus of the beast that was the prison, were the punishment cells known collectively as "el apando," or the hole. Located near the boilers, the hole was a prison within a prison, a box within a box within a box that contained more darkness and fear than would have seemed possible. No light reached this section of the penitentiary, just as no light reaches the entrails of a beast. The prisoners were kept in metal-lined cells with no toilet or sink; they were forced to piss and shit on the floor's metal plates, where their urine, feces, and diarrhea would gradually dry. There was a narrow slot in the door at chest height that could be opened only from outside, through which the guards could pass the prisoners something to eat once a day at most, though it could easily be every two or three days, and often they were given leftovers or food that had already gone bad. Spoiler: Martín and Nuria never spent time in these cells, but they heard about those who did. It was the most brutal space in the entire Black Palace, and the stories about it twisted and grew as they circulated, further proving, perhaps, how much fear the so-called asshole of the penitentiary provoked.

The woman with hair styled more perfectly than life itself and hands clasped behind her back led Nuria to have three photographs taken—one facing forward and two in profile, just like in the movies—as part of the bureaucracy surrounding her intake, to be filed with her full name and case number, followed by documentation of her conduct inside the penitentiary and her medical records. She also brought Nuria to pick up the two uniforms she was allotted: a skirt, a blouse, and a striped tunic, all made of coarse muslin. Nuria asked what she should do with the clothes she was wearing. Because her sentence was a long one, the woman with almost nonexistent lips and a gaze as black as a crow's told her that it was probably best to just throw them away. Prison employees were not allowed to engage the inmates in any kind of friendly chatter, but the woman with the dark gaze took this professional distance to another level entirely. She explained, with the detachment of a voiceover, that—like in Prussian prisons—in this, the most modern carceral facility in all of Mexico and the only maximum-security prison in the nation, upon their release prisoners are given a new, clean, decent suit or dress, courtesy of the state. Nuria threw her old clothing in the trash as if it were a handful of orange peels, as if her past would soon shrivel and decompose like something that might rot, sullying her present. On their way to the ward, the woman, still speaking like a voiceover, explained the rules of life inside.

In the prison yard, Nuria Valencia made eye contact with two women who were singing a ranchera—pretty well, to tell the truth—but as she and the woman whose hair looked like an open book got closer, the women stopped what they were doing and began to whisper amongst themselves. In her cell, Nuria observed the heavy blanket folded on the other bed and the belongings of the stranger who would be her cellmate. She peered at the toilet and, before she'd spent even three minutes inside, asked the woman with the straight part and the furrowed brow how much longer until she was released. Twenty years minus an hour and a half, replied the administrator with her arms crossed—and maybe her heart welded shut—before leaving Nuria alone.

Nuria Valencia and Martín Fernández had been able to secure legal counsel thanks to the fact that Lamadrid had taken the famous case pro bono after the couple's interrogation by Rubén Darío Hernández in the offices of Special Operations. The lawyer managed to ensure that Nuria would spend twenty years in prison, rather than forty, and secured the minimum sentence for Martín. He also represented Hortensia García García and advised Nuria's parents and Martín's mother. Lamadrid, with his elegant speech, his broad knowledge of the law, and the way he moved his fingers delicately in the air like a pianist as he spoke, giving greater authority to his words, made sure that the verdict was, in the end, as fair as possible. He argued that the law disfavored women, especially those women who desired to become mothers; that the process of adoption was labyrinthine and cruel; and that the public healthcare system was egregiously feeble in the areas of obstetrics and gynecology. The reporter Córdova wrote an article for his national newspaper about how certain laws were detrimental to women—a very forward-thinking piece for the time, it should be said—that got him called into his boss's office.

Ana María Felipe followed Nuria Valencia's case. She insisted that Beatriz make clippings of any mention of it and had read Nuria's statement to Rubén Darío Hernández about her reasons for doing what she did. She had even spoken on the phone with Lamadrid. That conversation, along with the text written by José Córdova, had indirectly sparked something in her: now that Nuria was in prison, somewhere deep inside her, somewhere tied to her own maternity, she found herself empathizing with the woman. She didn't approve of her crime—it was Ana María's granddaughter who had been the victim, after all—but she did understand Nuria's position, up to a point. She didn't discuss this with anyone, least of all her daughter, but every so often she would use her influence to inquire how Nuria was doing in prison. What would happen if she were to learn that Nuria needed something inside the Black Palace? Would she be willing to send her money? Anonymously, perhaps?

Nuria met Celeste, her cellmate. She didn't speak much at first, but over time she grew more comfortable. She was thirty-two years old and had several tattoos. Nuria hadn't seen many tattoos in her life, maybe just a few in the cardiologist's office, and she hadn't imagined that a woman could have one. Celeste had her parents' names and wedding date tattooed in a ribbon on one arm, and several different dates tattooed on the other under the image of a dove in flight. They'd been done by a kid who was locked up at Lecumberri, too. He went by El Conejo and was only fourteen years old; his artistic talent and the sheer number of tattoos he'd done on the inside kept him safe and earned him the respect of the other men deprived of liberty. El Conejo, who had a gap between his front teeth, got his name for being fast as a rabbit in the ring. He was in a boxing group and had a notebook where he drew his tattoo designs, some of which were of boxers. Celeste's tattoo was unusual. It came from a memory El Conejo had of a dove rising into the air in front of the church he attended with his parents when he was a little boy, back when he still prayed to God with his hands clasped. He had truly believed that the dove was God. Celeste told Nuria that El Conejo had tattooed the dove on her to bring her good luck when she got out, and that—looking like a juvenile thug with a gap between his front teeth—he'd said it was the most special tattoo he'd ever done. She talked about her other tattoos, but Nuria still didn't know why Celeste was there and it took a while to get her to open up; in contrast, rumors spread through the women's wards as soon as Nuria arrived, and another inmate had told Celeste the story of why Nuria was locked up, though that version was nowhere near the truth, after being distorted by so many mouths. One of those nights, Nuria and Celeste began to confide in one another. They still avoided talking about the past, but Celeste did hint at something when she said to Nuria, "We're here for the same reason, Mami. Because people with money want us in here. You haven't seen the writing out in the yard, have you? I don't remember it word for word but check it out. It's like the Lord's Prayer of this shithole, Mami." The next morning, as they passed through the prison yard on their way to the workshops, Celeste gave a quick nod in the direction of a few words scratched into its surface: "So you got sent to this hole to do time, / but don't forget what you're really in for: / it's not punishment for doing the crime, / it's punishment for being poor."

During her first three months in prison, Nuria suffered from anxiety and had two panic attacks, which afforded her two things: first, more empathy from her cellmate, who began taking care of her, and second, a chalky white pill that tasted bitter when it dissolved on her tongue. Nuria's second panic attack happened when she was in her cell. Celeste, in an attempt to calm her, asked what she had enjoyed in her life before she was sent to the Black Palace, and Nuria answered that she'd loved reading to her daughter at night. Celeste knew by then that she was talking about a daughter who wasn't her daughter and decided to share something important.

"You know what, Mami? I don't want kids, never have. Don't want nothing to do with them. I pray to God every night, I say, Don't even think about sending me any brats, and I cross myself three times to make sure he hears me . . ."

Nuria kept her eyes fixed on the ceiling as she asked her why not. Celeste gave her a long list of reasons that Nuria didn't entirely agree with, but in the end, she understood that Celeste really meant what she said. She wasn't interested. Plain and simple. That night marked their first intimate conversation, the first time they'd talked with a purpose other than exchanging information.

The next day, Celeste brought Nuria to the library and told her that she didn't know how to read. She'd gotten only as far as second grade and had always wanted to learn how, but the teacher assigned to her level had too many students to give her the attention required for someone with a head as hard as hers, as she said. She asked Nuria to help her. In their classes, the inmates could take notes about what the teacher said, but it wasn't a two-way street, and Celeste, who had dyslexia, needed personalized attention. Nuria agreed to teach Celeste to read and, in the process, threw together a small class of her own, a reading group made of up five women who needed individual attention. This initiative earned Nuria "privileges" from the administration, in the form of days taken off her sentence for each class she taught.

The first two women who signed up were the ones who had made eye contact with Nuria the day she arrived at the Black Palace. Elia and Leslie confessed that they'd been curious about her. They were joined by a woman known as "La Abuela" because at thirty-five years old, she'd already been incarcerated longer than any of the other female inmates and went around saying she was like a grandmother to all of them. She had a domineering personality and a loud voice to match her imposing stature; she filled every room she stepped into. The day after she signed up, La Abuela showed Nuria her strength in the mess hall, like a silverback in the mountains demonstrating his power to a younger ape; all the women called her Abue or Abuela, and she showed her upper gums as she grinned triumphantly at Nuria, like she did whenever she laughed. Next came Carmen, a woman of few words and a tiny voice that seemed to be wrapped around her bones as if she wanted to disappear. She was fifty-four years old and had committed a misdemeanor. I stole milk, she told the others during class one day, milk for my granddaughter. Leslie was twenty and

172

had been sent to the hole for selling drugs inside the penitentiary, which was also the reason she was sent to prison in the first place. She was usually withdrawn, as if she were trying to hide behind her bangs, but when she sang she stood tall and had a beautiful, forceful voice that didn't match her shy demeanor. Elia was twenty-seven and loved to sing, too, though she wasn't as good as Leslie. She was quick to laugh and loved to talk about illnesses she'd had over the course of her life and illnesses other inmates were suffering from, as if talking about illness could be a passion. Whenever anyone asked her how she was, she always had a list of aches and pains at the ready. With Nuria's help, the group read Aesop's fables and a few stories by the Brothers Grimm. During these sessions, between laughter and the occasional tear, they told stories from their pasts and shared how they'd ended up in the Black Palace.

Lecumberri's warden allowed Nuria to lead this class because not only was it producing results among the inmates, she was also one of the few inmates qualified to teach any of the workshops they offered, which reduced operating costs. Whoever taught these courses would receive a so-called reward that varied based on the situation and a positive note in their file about their assisting in their fellow inmates' reintegration into society. They were reading *The Ugly Duckling* when Nuria told the group how she used to read that story to her little girl and let something slip about the kidnapping of her daughter Agustina, which is what she called her in that moment. My daughter, Agustina. Carmen, the woman who had stolen milk, asked Nuria if she could give her a hug. The hug itself was stiff, but it was sincere and meant a lot to Nuria. Later on, she told Martín how important Carmen's gesture had been to her. She felt like she was making friends in there for the first time in her adult life, but Martín didn't feel the same way.

He felt lonely, actually. Leaving behind his life as he knew it had opened a hole in him that he still couldn't fully understand. He didn't really understand the new emotions he was discovering in prison, either, and didn't want to, but he was clear on the fact that he was angry with Nuria. How could she be making friends in this place? He felt like he couldn't connect with anyone, least of all with himself, as if prison had isolated him from himself, above all.

"You know what, Mami?" Celeste said to Nuria one night, almost whispering. "I never wanted to have kids. Even got rid of one that a guy I was seeing put in me." This conversation, during which Celeste described her clandestine abortion in detail, was like a breath of fresh air. The way she talked about it released something in Nuria: Celeste's aversion to motherhood felt like a weight being lifted from her shoulders or, rather, the swirl of air that follows a storm. Nuria asked herself for the very first time where she had gotten the idea that she needed to be a mother. Had it come from her? From society? Was it part and parcel of getting married? A mandate thrust upon her just because she'd been born a woman? The fresh breeze after a downpour feels so good on your face.

Nuria got the idea to do a dramatic reading of one of Aesop's fables, which really improved their progress and the dynamic among the group. She asked the women what they thought about presenting a few fables to the other inmates, like a play in a theater. This sparked commotion: the women began talking all at once about becoming famous actresses and joking about their breakout roles as dogs and birds. Most of all, they liked the idea of being seen by the other inmates, so that afternoon Nuria asked the prison administration for permission to stage a dramatic reading of Aesop's fables in the room where they held their reading class. The woman with the meticulous bun and the furrowed brow said they could, as long as they kept it to the same schedule when the group usually met and the activity didn't interfere with any of their other responsibilities at the prison. And that's how it came to be that one week later Nuria wrote a sign and posted it on the classroom door, and the women went around inviting people all morning to see them perform. All Nuria did to simulate a theater was to turn a few chairs so they were facing a wall: the stage. That magic, the simple act that makes the fiction possible. There were a total of nine people in the audience, including Martín, who watched his wife direct the activity. Annoyed, a bit resentful, and a bit surprised to see her interact with the other women, he wondered how Nuria had accomplished all this. Had being further from her overprotective parents allowed her to make friends? "TODAY! Two fables by Aesop" read the sign on the door.

First, they did a staged reading of "The Tortoise and the Hare." They invented dialogues: La Abuela was a chatty hare, and Celeste a foul-mouthed tortoise. A few comments from the audience hurt La Abuela's feelings, for example, when the two characters race one another, one of the guys known for getting sent to the hole started making fun of her body. "I want some of what they feed that hare! All we get for breakfast around here is atole, but she's gotta be getting something on the side, look at her!" Nuria tried to restore order, but two of the audience members, who thought it was ridiculous that animals were speaking from the uniformed bodies of prison inmates, kept heckling the women. Three people walked in late. The second reading was of "The Grasshopper and the Ant." Leslie sang a song as the grasshopper. Someone whistled along. They didn't heckle Elia and Leslie as much, but the same guy who'd made a comment about La Abuela said how stupid it was to watch two insects talking. Martín and two other people who showed up late applauded wildly, which the women

175

liked—especially Carmen, who hadn't really participated but who received the praise as if it were meant for her, simply for being part of the reading group. It was the first time in all her fifty-four years that someone had given her a round of applause, and it felt great, especially when she met Nuria's eyes as she clapped for her. No one had ever done that before.

At the next class, they talked about how the performance had gone. Everyone had really liked how three of the other inmates had clapped for them; Carmen wasn't alone in that. The one who applauded loudest was a "joto," said La Abuela, trying to minimize his appreciation of Leslie. But the group talked about how good La Abuela's acting had been, and Nuria noticed that it was the first time they were really talking about the content of the fables they'd read in class, all because they wanted to make La Abuela feel like she'd gotten applause, too. Following an impulse, an intuition, Nuria decided to propose that they put on a whole play. Celeste and La Abuela were on board, though they didn't know what putting on a play involved; in fact, La Abuela had a proposal of her own: "If we're gonna be famous actresses and shit, we should call ourselves the Grandbabies, so everyone knows who my bitches answer to." Everyone thought that was pretty funny, and that was how the troupe came to have a name before it had official permission to exist and long before it staged its first play.

Nuria spoke to the woman with the middle part, eyes like a rainstorm, and almost nonexistent lips. She asked for permission to stage a play at the end of the month. The woman brought her to her superior, and Nuria convinced him. That same afternoon, she stopped by the library to see what plays they had in the prison. The library clerk, who had very bad breath, showed her to a small section. Nuria was there for a while before selecting a copy of Shakespeare's *Hamlet* with a few pages missing from between its battered covers, which were like an article of clothing that had been patched and patched again over the patches, and a play by Federico García Lorca. Because she was a teacher, the prison library clerk—why was his breath so bad? What had he eaten or drunk that smelled so much like death warmed over?—allowed her to take the volumes back to her cell. The members of this troupe with a name but no play to perform were excited by the prospect of being seen by more inmates. What if five or ten of them clapped? Or even fifteen? Carmen was especially enthusiastic about this prospect and wanted to participate. Elia asked if they'd be allowed to wear makeup and costumes for the play.

Over the course of a few days, between whispered nighttime conversations with Celeste, Nuria Valencia leafed through *Hamlet* and the play by Federico García Lorca. Celeste was asleep when Nuria read the first pages of *Yerma*, which Lorca had published in 1934 and by then had been staged in various theaters in Spain and beyond. By the end of the first scene, Nuria was hooked. When she finished the play, a few tears ran down her cheeks as she thought about what she'd just read; she wiped them away with the back of one hand as the other still held *Yerma* open to its final pages. This was the play they would perform.

Nuria told the women what this play with short and beautiful dialogues was about. At the beginning, Yerma has been married to Juan for two years and is desperate to have a child with him, though he doesn't feel this need as urgently. Time passes and her desire to be a mother remains unfulfilled; her relationship with her husband begins to sour at the same pace as her relationship with the world. Juan suggests that they adopt one of their nephews, but Yerma doesn't like the idea, because what she wants is to give birth to the child she will raise. Deep down, she thinks that if she had married her first love, Víctor, she wouldn't be childless.

It becomes clear that Yerma doesn't love Juan: her father arranged their marriage, and an old woman tells her that this lack of love might the reason behind their inability to start a family. Juan realizes that people in town are talking about them and brings his two sisters home with him to keep an eye on his wife. Yerma goes to see a semi-witch who reveals to her that Juan is the reason she can't bear children. Juan loves Yerma, he's deeply in love with his wife, and one night, when she looks particularly beautiful under the full moon, he tries to sleep with her. Just before his desire is fulfilled, however, Yerma strangles him to death. The first thing Celeste asks Nuria is what *Yerma* means. "Is that name for real, Mami? They go around Spain naming girls Yerma López and shit like that?" All the women liked the play and, one way or another, they all sensed a connection to their own crimes.

Nuria read the play to them out loud, and they divided up the roles. The five women would play both the male and the female roles, obviously. Nuria was in charge and would direct the play. Celeste would star as Yerma and La Abuela would play Juan. Carmen would have two roles: the old woman and the semi-witch. Elia and Leslie would be Juan's sisters. Among the five, they would take turns with secondary roles like the washwomen, though Leslie would sing the washwomen's songs as a soloist. They weren't allowed to change out of their prison uniforms, but Nuria had the idea to request some newspapers from the wardens and ask Carmen, who was good at crafts, to make a skirt for Yerma by folding pleats into the paper and a newspaper hat for Juan, like the kind construction workers wore. A newspaper moustache and beard for Pastor Víctor; newspaper veils for Juan's sisters; and newspaper aprons for the washwomen who gossiped about the ins and outs of Yerma and Juan's marriage. Carmen was deeply grateful to the group for trusting her not only with two roles in the play, but also with its wardrobe, to which she would dedicate herself with care.

The Grandbabies began selecting key scenes and boiling the play down to the parts that resonated most with them. They adapted certain things and cut a few of Lorca's verses; they laughed at some of the lines and adapted the dialogue as they saw fit. Nuria requested three things of the administration: ten old newspapers so Carmen could make their costumes; a loan of the two wooden screens from the office for the actresses to stand behind before going onstage, like being in the wings of a theater; and—this was her most complicated request—two fifteen-foot poles for the day of the performance, to make stage curtains out of fabric from the other workshops. Nuria explained what she planned to do with each item to the head warden, who asked her to fill out a form and wait several days for a response.

Nuria spent most of her time in the women's cell block and in her routines inside the prison, but she also got to see Martín from time to time. They were even allowed conjugal visits. Every two weeks, in an open space divided only by sheets, on a bare floor without even a mattress or a mat, a few couples were permitted this kind of visit. There was no privacy whatsoever in this encampment of sheets and blankets, and among the sounds of groaning and flesh meeting and parting and meeting again, Martín and Nuria caught up with one another—pretending, for the guards, that they were having sex. They also talked about how they felt, what they were doing with their days. By then Martín had already told Nuria that he'd figured out what was going on a few months after the little girl arrived, but that he had wanted the life they were living, too, and had decided not to say anything. They didn't have sex during these conjugal visits, but they did reach a new level of intimacy. It was the closest thing they had to privacy, even though there was really nothing private about it, and that allowed Martín to approach Nuria differently than he had before, despite the resentment he still felt toward her. They had almost had sex during a conjugal visit when the Grandbabies were rehearsing Lorca's *Yerma*, but Martín hadn't been able to get it up. Nuria managed to tell Martín—who was pleased, on one hand, to see her excited for the first time in a long while, but who also felt it was unfair—that she had requested ten newspapers and two wooden screens and a pair of rods for curtains to stage the play, and that she was almost positive it was going to come together. She was animated, even happy. Martín asked her if she needed any help, knowing full well that Lecumberri's rules made his helping her just as impossible as his getting an erection.

When they were first locked up, Martín was angry at Nuria. Which is to say, he was furious. He didn't talk to her. He regretted not mentioning the situation with the girl long before, so many lives ago. He'd known exactly what had happened; he didn't know how Nuria had done it and didn't dare to ask, but he understood. He saw the newspapers on his way home from work. He heard his colleagues' radios at the office. He knew that "his daughter" was the Miranda Felipe girl. But he decided to play dumb, as his cellmate said, because Nuria was happy and—this became clearer to him in Lecumberri—he was, too. Seeing her happy again because of the play she was putting on made him feel strange . . . Did he feel better? He wasn't sure, but at least he was more at peace than when they got there.

In the room where they would stage the play, Nuria Valencia fantasized about a different space. She suddenly dreamt about performing it in a theater, a space with seats lined up in a darkness that would divide the fiction from reality, that would serve the play with its light and its shadows, that would reveal the fiction within the reality and all their complicity, but her life was happening in that overlit prison room. Her life was a yawning present that saw all in those cell blocks and those rooms where bright lights illuminated—and vigilant eyes watched—absolutely everything. And if her life was happening there, why couldn't a play, too? Couldn't fiction happen anywhere? The administration approved the ten old newspapers and the two wooden screens, for the day of the performance only; the two rods were also approved for the day, on the condition that a junior guard be there to keep an eye on them. Nuria was waiting for the group when Carmen arrived, right on time.

In this rehearsal, Nuria realized that instead of using the two rods to hold pieces of fabric like a stage curtain, they could be used to indicate the play's emotional backdrop. From one of the rods, held up by a woman at either end, would hang strips of fabric in blues, grays, and whites that would wave like melancholy rainfall, as a way to suggest natural light in the background and mark the sad moments of the play; the more hopeful moments, the warmer, lighter, funnier moments, would be marked by a background of red, orange, and yellow strips rippling from the other rod. Much of Lorca's poetry would be waving in those strips of fabric. The two screens—this was Carmen's great idea—could serve not just as wings and dressing rooms, but also as scenery: they could cover them with cardboard to protect the wood and paint some mountains, a big round sun like a child would paint, and Yerma and Juan's house somewhere off to the side.

As the performance drew nearer, the connection between the Grandbabies grew, and it grew livelier. The women memorized their lines and practiced them as they went about their duties and routines in the penitentiary. When they ran into one another in the hallways, they would chat, wonder, and laugh as they speculated about what would happen on the day. "From el apando all the way to the silver screen," La Abuela would say, her guffaw drowning out all other laughter. A few days before, Nuria stuck a sign she'd made to the door of the room: "*Yerma* by Federico García Lorca, performed by the Grandbabies, Saturday at noon. In this room. Please be punctual."

Nuria had a dream the night before they performed the play: she was in a pool like one she'd seen outside a house in Morelos near her father's hardware store, a house with palms, orange trees, and banana plants that gave off the most delicious smell on summer nights. She was alone in that pool and in that house, which she'd never set foot inside but had always wondered about as she passed. Everything smelled good, felt good. The water seemed to be there just to please her. It changed temperature, and she enjoyed being in the warmer water even more. Happy, Nuria moved around a little and discovered that she could change the water's temperature with her movements. She could also make it smell more intensely of orange blossom, her favorite scent, just by wiggling her fingers. But how could it be that not only was she free, but she could also control the temperature of the water, the intensity of the perfumes wafting from the trees, and the color of the sky, making its pink turn violet with orange over here, magenta over there, and yellow at the edge? What was that? Nuria awoke with her arms moving under her heavy blanket, unsettled by the contrast between her current reality and the water in her dream, her sense of well-being.

How was it possible that Nuria could feel good inside the prison that day? That she could feel so good. Free, even. Free from working. Free from shopping. Free from having to be a good wife. Free from having to be a mother. Free from having to be a good daughter. Free from having to be the woman that society expected.

182

Free from having to be somebody. Free to be who she was. How could it be that Nuria felt so free that day in prison as she made her way to the performance of *Yerma*.

The Grandbabies were waiting in the wings behind wooden screens painted with mountains, in their muslin uniforms and newspaper costumes. The room was full and out of control: whistles, laughter, hijinks, people talking over each other. Nuria was close to the door waiting for the junior guard who was supposed to bring the two rods with the strips of colorful fabric, when another guard walked in, shouting, "All right, shut up, you sons of bitches" while banging on the wall with his nightstick. The guard Nuria had been waiting for followed him in and handed her the rods with the strips of fabric. Nuria helped two women from the unit who had volunteered to lift the sticks according to the mood of the scene, friends of Leslie's who had attended the final rehearsal, to get the rods positioned correctly on the floor. The woman with the perfectly parted hair entered the room, arms crossed, followed by the prison library clerk. They got everyone to settle down and the play began.

Something strange happened: after the first few lines of dialogue between Yerma and Juan, no one in the audience made another sound. Nuria watched the first scene between the married couple from near the door in the back of the room. In the second scene, Carmen—in her role as the old woman, with a hood made of newsprint—told Celeste in her newspaper skirt: "We should desire our men, my girl. They should loosen our braids and let us sip water straight from their mouths because that's what makes the world go 'round," while strips of red, orange, and yellow fabric fluttered in the background. A man whistled in approval and another yelled, "You said it!" They were shouting at the characters, rather than the actresses? What was going on? Yerma continued, saying that she wasn't attracted to her husband, that the man she desired was Pastor Víctor. Yerma argued with Juan: "But I'm not you. Men have another life, you tend cattle, cut wood, you ride out on the ranch; all women get to do is have babies and raise them." A little while later, Leslie sang. Someone coughed in the corner, but everyone was captivated by the play, even the guards and the members of the prison administration, whom Nuria was watching from the corner of one eye. At the end of the third and final act, when Juan tries to sleep with Yerma and she kills him, Nuria began to cry, but she didn't notice it, as if her body were acting independently of her. She realized she was crying only when she met Martín's eyes and he made a gesture to ask if she was all right. Maybe the tears had come because it frees the spirit to see yourself reflected in a play. Applause, whistles; someone shouted, "That Yerma's one bad broad!" and the room erupted in applause all over again. Celeste, La Abuela, Carmen, Elia, and Leslie stepped out to take a bow. One woman yelled, "You're an asshole, Juan!" at La Abuela. Three men in the front row applauded energetically, one of them directly at Carmen, while another raised two fingers to his mouth to whistle his fury straight at Yerma.

The next day, Celeste told Nuria that some inmates had approached her in the yard as if she were Yerma, and La Abuela, who had joined them in the mess hall, told them that something similar had happened to her, that even at that early hour a few people had already yelled "Fucking Juan!" at her. On Tuesday, the administrator with the dark gaze and arched eyebrows sent for Nuria Valencia. She told her that the warden was instructing them to perform the play again on Saturday because other administrators, including one of the prison's directors, wanted to attend, and because several inmates who had missed the original performance had requested to see it. In the mess hall, Nuria began getting piloncillo in her coffee, one of the privileges she gained by putting on the play. Sweetened coffee, a thing only a handful of inmates in the entire prison got to enjoy, was a sign that everything had gone better than well.

Nuria and Martín were in Lecumberri for a long time before they were able to have sex in those conjugal visits, which they usually used for catching up with one another. Those encounters were the closest thing they had to their room in their house at 31 Calle Violeta in Colonia Guerrero, which had come to feel as distant as a whisper. For Nuria, it had been hard at first to overcome her anxiety, her panic attacks, and the white pills that robbed her of her libido. Martín, for his part, was uneasy and convinced he wouldn't be able to finish. The knowledge that he could be seen and heard inhibited him, just as he was generally subdued by the feeling of being watched at every moment. In all those months, he had masturbated only once. While his cellmate snored, he thought about an actress who had once come to the film offices where he worked: she was wearing a low-cut dress that framed her breasts and had strikingly full hips, but he could have masturbated looking at the ceiling of his cell or closing his eyes in total darkness while thinking about nothing at all. When he finally did have sex with Nuria during one of those visits, he came right away, leaving her little time for anything.

A few weeks later, in the reading group where Nuria Valencia now had twenty-five students, six of them were practicing a dramatic reading of one of Aesop's fables, improvising possible dialogues between the animals. When Nuria handed the book to La Abuela, who wasn't participating, La Abuela peered at her and then pulled her close. "You're pregnant," she whispered. "Look at the sparkle in your eyes." No one had ever said anything like that to Nuria, and she knew it wasn't true—she knew, in fact, that it wasn't possible, but La Abuela insisted. "Look at your eyes! They're sparkling like a pregnant critter's." Nuria told her quietly that she was sterile, putting an end to the conversation, and got back to the group. La Abuela exchanged a glance with Celeste, who gestured for her to leave Nuria alone.

Nuria's period was late by a few weeks, so she went to the infirmary to tell the doctor that she thought she was going through menopause. The doctor replied that it was quite possible, that many women went through menopause earlier than expected in that place. It's more common at your age than you'd think, he said, without taking his eyes from a folder he was closing on his desk. Then he opened Nuria's file, which was already on hand. He leafed through it. The best course of action would be a hysterectomy, he said from the other side of his desk, before this becomes a problem for you and for the prison. We'll rid you of the discomfort of early menopause, it's a win-win, he said, looking straight at her. The doctor began filling out a form with Nuria's information, asked her a few questions to update her medical file, and insisted that it had been a mistake not to have children earlier, because— in his words—there was no turning back, now. He was going to give her a checkup to fill in a few remaining fields on the form. When was her last period? How was her health, generally? Could she identify the cause of the vomiting she had reported, perhaps something she ate? Probably just a side effect of the menopause. Any hot flashes? Her diagnosis of infertility and the treatment to unblock her Fallopian tubes, when had all that been? The doctor decided to examine Nuria. It was, without a doubt, a case of early menopause. He would need urine and blood samples to complete his report and order the hysterectomy so they could remove her uterus in the operating room next door sometime in the next few days.

When the doctor told Nuria Valencia that a hysterectomy was out of the question because she was pregnant, she shifted in her seat three times. Nuria seemed unable to find a position she could remain in, as if she had forgotten how to sit, how to be. She waited a few seconds, clasped her hands on the doctor's desk, and asked him how that was possible. The doctor replied that he couldn't explain it, but that the tests confirmed a pregnancy, and that a hysterectomy was out of the question. Nuria didn't know what to do with her arms, or her legs, or her body, and so she began to play with her thumbs, to make circles with them as if her entire body, and, while we're at it, her entire life were expressed by that movement.

Leaving the doctor's office, Nuria paused in the hall of skulls and stared for a moment at the tiniest ones. She didn't know what to do with her body, but there it was, able to move all by itself, to carry her places she hadn't asked it to, and so she took those sockets with her eyes in them for a walk, taking everything in; everything was so different now, she was so different now, so different from what she'd thought she was, pregnant at her age. The first person she told about her pregnancy was La Abuela, who was in the yard talking with El Conejo while he did boxing drills with his hands wrapped. Nuria pulled her aside and gave her the news in two words. La Abuela, showing her upper gums as she laughed, cried "My girl!" and immobilized Nuria with a hug. Then Nuria went to find Martín; she told Celeste that night.

When Nuria Valencia Pérez's parents learned of their daughter's pregnancy during visiting hours, her mother fell to her knees, closed her eyes, and recited one Ave Maria after another until her words became a rosary while her father listened attentively. When they told Martín's mother, she asked, "What are you going to do, son?" as if the pregnancy were Nuria's alone, or as if he were the only one in prison. José Córdova was the first to publish an article about Nuria's pregnancy and brought a photographer from the newspaper named Guerrero with him to the Black Palace to take the only picture that exists of Nuria Valencia pregnant in her prison uniform. More people read that article than any other in the evening edition, and the media picked up the case again. The news was discussed on several radio programs, and Ana María Felipe got wind of the story. Deep down, she felt happy when she saw the photograph.

Over the course of her pregnancy, Nuria had sex with Martín often during their conjugal visits. A reporter interviewed four of the many gynecologists who had declared Nuria infertile, asking them to explain how, in their professional opinion, this could have happened. Each one of them said that there was no medical explanation for it. Agustina Mendía was given the article by a neighbor of hers, a fervent Catholic who felt she should be aware that her future grandchild was a Miracle of God, but after reading it Agustina set the newspaper on the dining room table and took a long bath, even though it was still early afternoon.

That night, at a party hosted by a famous film director, Ana María found herself conversing with two women who brought up the topic of Nuria Valencia falling pregnant inside Lecumberri. The only time Ana María ever allowed herself to speak honestly about the pregnancy of the woman who had kidnapped her granddaughter was with that pair of strangers. "A child is always a blessing," she said. In contrast, she addressed the topic in monosyllabic words with her daughter and avoided it entirely with her son-in-law. As Nuria's due date approached, Ana María—using her wealth and connections, as usual—had her chauffeur drive Beatriz to the Black Palace with a gift. It arrived on the day Nuria gave birth. A gown made of raw silk, just like the ones that would soon sell like hotcakes in her new children's clothing shop, so that the baby could be christened inside the penitentiary, holy water in a milk bottle, a small white Bible, and a letter written on Florentine paper that only Nuria read. Martín had no interest in reading it, nor did he pay much attention when Nuria told him that Ana María was in a relationship with a fabric manufacturer, and little Gloria Miranda Felipe had named two of her dolls Martín and Nuria. In her letter, Ana María also thanked Nuria for taking such good care of her granddaughter.

Eva Fernández Valencia was born after twenty hours of labor in Lecumberri's operating room, at 3:32 a.m. She weighed seven pounds and three ounces and was healthy and all in one piece, though the first thing Martín did when they put him in her arms was to count her fingers and toes, since his cellmate had told him that because his wife was so old—thirty-seven—there was a chance some would be missing. Eva had been in the world for just a few hours, with her eyes still closed and her face all swollen, when Martín said to Nuria, "She looks just like my mother."

That night, Nuria slept with her baby on her chest. How? How could this be? How could this have happened? How could there be words for this? How could there be words for all this, in here? How could there be words for all she'd seen, all she'd lived? For all she'd felt? How could she put it all into words? How could she say it? How?

The Grandbabies got together to write a letter to President Miguel Alemán and the directors of Lecumberri requesting the immediate release of Nuria Valencia Pérez so she could watch her daughter Eva Fernández Valencia grow up outside the prison. This letter was leaked to the press, and the spirited debate it sparked made it all the way to Gloria Felipe, who had intentionally been ignoring the newspapers. She called her mother, who pretended to know nothing about it. "No, really?" replied Ana María over the phone. Gloria Felipe asked her for a name at the appellate court, which she received. She presented a letter requesting that Nuria Valencia not be released immediately from prison because she had committed a crime that could not and should not go unpunished, but stating that she would be amenable to a reduction of her sentence.

Many words were spoken, then more words, and then more. They traveled like waves and broke in whites, blues, and brilliant flashes. Lamadrid exerted pressure, strengthened their case. The judge heard arguments. One afternoon several months later, after the verdict had been announced—Martín would serve one more year; Nuria, four—and after the couple had trusted Eva to the care of Gonzalo and Carmela, it began to rain. Nuria needed to cross the round prison yard and didn't want to get soaked, so she began to run. And the rain fell harder, she felt it trickling down her body and smelled it in the air, and—what can the rain offer anyone?—as she smelled the fat drops hitting the ground and soaking her muslin uniform, Nuria knew she was pregnant again.

Mexico City
October 2023

With Gratitude

To Michel Lipkes. Thank you for making this story better; most of all, thank you for making my life better. Respect, admiration, and love.

To my family. To my brother Diego, whom I adore and admire. To my father. Special thanks to Gloria, my mother, and the maternal lineage she gave me. To my grandfather Gustavo (1926–2012) and my grandmother Gloria (1927–2009) and my badass great-grandmother Ana María (1906–1996), who are with me wherever I go.

To my friends, thank you for reading early drafts, for accompanying me in this process, for the conversations I had with each of you. This book exists thanks to: Gabriela Jauregui, Elena Fortes, Luis Felipe Fabre, Vera Félix, Catherine Lacey, Laura Gandolfi, Gabriel Kahan, Heather Cleary, Tania Pérez Córdova, Julieta Venegas, Camila de Iturbide, Tania Lili, Mariana Barrera, Valeria Luiselli, Elvira Liceaga, Fernando Gómez Candela, Lilyana Torres, Martina Spataro, Paula Amor, Marcos Castro, Karla Kaplun, Regina Serratos, Carlos Azar, and Mauro Libertella. My thanks to Lourdes Valdés. And to José Leandro Córdova Lucas

(I borrowed your name for a character in this book, just like I did in the first book I wrote, at twenty-three, and in *Witches*, which has a character named Leandra in it) for the long walks we took and have yet to take, and because I still write today feeling the love and support that you gave me. To my admired teacher, the medievalist Gloria Prado, who recommended poems and readings to me during the pandemic to help me think about the use of the third person.

I wrote this novel with the support of the Albert & Elaine Borchard Foundation; I am especially grateful to Michael Spurgeon. I am also deeply grateful to each and every one of my colleagues at *El País* for our conversations about the topics we cover. Special thanks to Héctor Guerrero, Javier Lafuente, Sonia Corona, and David Marcial Pérez. To Nayeli García, Fernanda Álvarez, Mayra González, the three editors at Alfaguara with whom I worked on this book, and to Pedro Salamanca for his reading of it. To Carina Pons, Jorge Manzanilla, Laura Palomares, and everyone at the Carmen Balcells Agency. And to Kendall Storey and the amazing team at Catapult. It is a privilege to work with each and every one of you. Thank you.

© Ana Hop

BRENDA LOZANO is a fiction writer, essayist, and editor. Her books include *Todo nada* (All or Nothing), followed by *Cuaderno ideal* (*Loop*), the book of short stories *Cómo piensan las piedras* (How Stones Think), and *Brujas* (*Witches*). She is part of the celebrated Bogotá39 among the best Latin American writers, lives in Mexico City, and writes for *El País*.

© Walter Funk

HEATHER CLEARY is an award-winning translator whose work has been recognized by the National Book Foundation, the Queen Sofía Spanish Institute, and English PEN, among other organizations.